Remembrance

THE POETRY OF THE ZADOKIM

Cassondra E. Beers

Eyedentified Publishing Solutions, SPRINGDALE, ARKANSAS

Library of Congress Control Number: 2017912039

Eyedentified Consulting Services, LLC
d/b/a Eyedentified Publishing Solutions
P.O. Box 6892
Springdale, AR 72766-6892
www.eyedentifiedconsulting.com

Book Layout © 2015 BookDesignTemplates.com

Publisher's Cataloging-In-Publication Data
(Prepared by The Donohue Group, Inc.)

Names: Beers, Cassondra E.
Title: Remembrance : the poetry of the Zadokim / Cassondra E. Beers.
Description: 1st ed. | Springdale, Arkansas : Eyedentified Publishing Solutions, [2017]
Identifiers: ISBN 978-1-945566-03-5 (paperback) | ISBN 978-1-945566-04-2 (hardcover) | ISBN 978-1-945566-05-9 (Kindle) | ISBN 978-1-945566-06-6 (ePub)
Subjects: LCSH: God (Christianity)--Promises--Poetry. | Presence of God--Poetry. | Memory--Religious aspects--Christianity--Poetry. | Christian poetry.
Classification: LCC PS3602.E47 R46 2017 (print) | LCC PS3602.E47 (ebook) | DDC 811/.6--dc23

May everyone remember their Promise.

CONTENTS

In the Beginning

In the Beginning, I and the Father were One. All that He knew that was related to me, I knew as well. I knew Him. I knew who I was. I knew the incontrovertible immutability of His love. I knew His plan for creation and my role in it. I knew when I would be born, the family into which I would be given. I knew the number of my days and the purposes for which I would be placed in the Earth. I knew the people I would relate to, the talents I would have, the family I would create. I knew the day I would leave the perception of the Earth again.

I knew the struggles I would go through: the wondering if anyone could ever love me, the depression, the fear of rejection, the thoughts that I was worthy only of death. I knew the physical weight I would gain, and the process of losing it again. I knew the day I would be healed of these things and that healing was not an instantaneous event. I knew that, sometimes, healing would be the most difficult thing of all. That was ok, because I also knew something else.
I knew the Promise of my Father.

I knew more than I know now, for I am only twenty-eight. Though I have experienced some of my life, and heard some of the Promises for my future, I have not seen every microsecond of my natural existence as I knew then in the Beginning.

I have, in my relationship with Yahweh, begun to remember certain things. My first anthology, *Promises: The Poetry of the Zadokim*, details some of the first things that Yahweh reminded me about myself and creation. The closer I grow to Yahweh, the more I remember. It is a joy to walk with Him again and become more and more One with Him again, discovering in the process all that He promised me when He spoke me into existence.

Before I was created, He laid my life out before me and He gave me a choice. It was not a command, to "Be!" but an option, "Let there be." I remember, now, saying "Yes and amen," and agreeing to Become.
"Let there be…"

And I was born, and all was as He said. My life unfolded as He had purposed in the Beginning, though I did not always know it. It unfolds still, and as I sit here typing and remembering who I am, what was in the Beginning, I know there is still so much more to discover of Yahweh's original plan and Promise for my life.

Sometimes it is a struggle to remember His Promises. The enemy loves nothing more than to veil Yahweh's Truth with darkness and lies and fear. Yet, the more I remember of Yahweh, the more I remember that the enemy truly has no power over me. Yahweh has reminded me. **The enemy does not have the power to remove the resources or break the Promises of Yahweh.**

So I will remember. I will remember who Yahweh has made me. Yahweh said, "Let there be" me, and I shall continue to, by faith, be.

Thanks for reading!
Cassondra

R e m e m b e r

A Remembrance

Once before time in a land beyond space,
I lived with my Father in a Heavenly place
I walked in the spirit in the cool of the day
The voice of my Father and His heartbeat held sway

I knew who I was and I knew why I lived
I lived in my Father and received all He gives
I saw everything that my life would be
I dwelled in Yahweh and He dwelled in me

I was told what would come and I saw time's expanse
I moved with my Father in a divine dance
We worked closely together as He planned my life
I knew what was coming when I chose to die

He warned me what would happen, what I would go through
But He made me a Promise and His Promise is true
He said He would love me with a love without end
Then sent me into the tapestry what was broken to mend

Then I came to the Earth and forgot everything
I forgot who I was, forgot Yahweh my King
I was born into sadness, into sin and doubt
I learned fear and madness; I learned to do without

For I had a great power as the child of the King
With the words that I spoke, I could create things
My Father's authority was given to me
But only if I could have His eyes to see

I was lost, I was hopeless, I was broken inside
But my Father's true Promise was surely alive
He came back to get me, He found me again
He gave me the grace to remember Him

As I grew to remember who my Father was
I also grew stronger in faith, hope, and love
I learned once again that I am me
My eyes have been opened and now I see

And though I'm still growing and remembering more
My Father, through my Brother, did open the door
He gave me a vision, He graced me with power
To bring His Promise to Earth, to bring life in this hour

If I can remember and can truly see
The Promise my Father has spoken to me
What He whispered in my ear when He spoke me to life
What He created for me and placed deep inside,

Mysteries hidden for me shall soon be unveiled
As I walk with my Father and His glory prevails
So again I will worship in the cool of the day
And rest in my Father, be with Him always

I will grow and keep growing until I'm complete
But always with a knowing that His Promise He keeps
And I will remember who I've always been
And see the completion of my Father's vision.

Remember

Mysteries

A world that I come from, this isn't my home
A place I've forgotten that I've always known
It isn't far from me, for it's not without
I cannot lose it; it's mine without doubt

If I look deep inside me, it's already there
A whole revelation, the universe's prayer
Hidden within me and part of my being
Such great revelation of mysterious things

Yahweh, Great Creator, did make mysteries
He planted in each of us a puzzle piece
A thread of creation, a line in a poem
A Word in a sentence, a Promise of Hope

We are the mysteries we must uncover
Then we can take these Truths and give to each other
And we bring Creation together as one
As we take our places in what Yahweh's done

So I'm on a journey and you're on one too
To discover inside us Yahweh's hidden Truths
But we're not to worry or to be afraid
For Yahweh has promised to be with us always

The joy of discovery, mysteries known
As Yahweh is faithful to carry us home
He walks beside us, the burden to bear
He gives us the Promise that we can all share

The love of the Father, His joy and His peace
The purpose inside us, our reason for being
Prosperity's Promise and all that He is
That we shall move forward receiving to give.

Remember

Revelation

Unveiling of the Promises that Yahweh made to us
Like the unwrapping of a present newly given
Squeals of delight, remembering that you are truly loved
Marveling at the new and joyful Presence

Knowing what your heart once knew but long ago forgot
When the Promise of the Father first was broken
Yet, even in the brokenness nothing was ever lost
Nothing can stop a Word once Yahweh's spoken

Hidden in pieces throughout time, scattered throughout space
Each piece containing facets of the Christ
Waiting for us to uncover them and then fully embrace,
The blessing comes with each piece that we find

Yet even though in pieces, Christ is Christ and He brings grace
Each piece contains the sum and total power
For you cannot diminish Him who inhabits every place,
Broke infinite-eternity into hours

The power of Christ is here for us, given once again
If we submit to the Holy Spirit's Promise
He sent us on a great adventure to rediscover Him
Knowing we never truly can be lost

The faith of Yahweh's truly great to send us on this mission
For He trusts that to Him we will return
If I did not return to Yahweh, I would always miss Him
I could not live without His Holy Word

Grateful for the Father's choice and for the Father's faith
That He would always find us where He sent us
And when we're tempted to forget, we can see Yahweh's grace
In hiding Himself in pieces so to mend us.

Remember
___

Signs and Wonders

Any time a person tells you
What they are believing for
Long before it happens
And then tells you when it has happened
That it is exactly what they were believing for
And more.

A Whisper

A soft, caressing breeze blows through the leaves of trees
The gentle flow of water over rocks and over streams
The sound of children's laughter, snow falling on the ground
The truth inside a line of verse, the meaning behind the sound

There are whispers all around you
Of what has always been
Yahweh fully surrounds you
And He calls you to enter in

Hidden in the voices, in the clamoring and shouts
Louder than all the noises and the feelings and the doubts
Stronger than all the shadows and the temporary things
The whisper of a Promise in a butterfly's new wings

Yahweh calls you to remember
What He told you before time
Inside you, sparks and embers
Are beginning to ignite

As He gently leads you onward and uncovers what was hidden
Your spirit will remember what He spoke to you in Heaven
But you shall not see the glory if you do not want to believe
You will never hold your vision unless you open your eyes to see

He shall help you in this purpose
He has not left you alone
He came to the Earth to get us
He will surely guide us home

In the paths that we will walk, Yahweh's whispering to us
Through the things that He created and in every time we love
He reminds us of the Promise that He'd spoken before time
Who we are, what the world is, the whole picture of our lives

He reminds me who I am
Who I've always, always been
He reminds me of the land
In which He's given me to live

I will listen for the whisper, I will not forget the voice
The One who called me into being, the One who gave to me a choice
For I can choose now to listen and I can choose to believe
Or I can give up the vision, walk away, live without peace

I will choose my Father
For my Father's chosen me
I consider it an honor
Now to give Him everything

The greatness of my Creator, Father, God, Yahweh, my King
Is that He can take the broken things and use them still to speak
One day Yahweh's gentle whisper will become a mighty shout
It grows louder, ever louder, as we conquer fear and doubt

For when things become unbroken
Yahweh's voice will more abound
All the Promises He's spoken
Throughout creation will resound

Every time that we remember what the Father said to us
We make His voice grow louder, coming together as one
With one voice we shall sing clearly of the Father's Promises
Everyone will be able to hear it and now make the choice to live

For by choosing paths of righteousness
Instead of wandering around,
We can share in Yahweh's Promise
And turn the whisper to a shout.

Voices

Clamoring voices, competing words
Strong contradictions of the Promise I've heard
Horrible circumstances, turmoil within
Violence and trials and great, rampant sin

Daily reminders that I'm not enough
Trying to drown out Yahweh's perfect love
Trying to bring awful fear to the front
Trying to cause me to quit and give up

But I am a Promise and I am a Word
The enemy can't stop the truth that I've heard
For once I believed it, it was part of me
And this is what Yahweh always meant to be

So though daily the voices may try to arise,
Trying to haunt me and fill me with lies,
Against the Promise of the Father nothing can compete
For His Word is just perfect and it is complete

So I simply rest now in His fulfilled Word
For He has established it, fully assured
He placed it inside me when He spoke me to life
So now I will live it and through Him I shine.

Remember

Perspective

Standing outside, looking at the sky
Asking my Father lots of questions
I don't understand, confusion is at hand
And I wonder if I have the right perspective

The world is confusing; Babylon's dumb
The chaos that surrounds me is exhausting
There is blindness about, making me want to shout
And so I bring my Father my true offering

I really can't say why people act that way
But then I guess I really shouldn't judge
I used to be there, mean because I was scared
I didn't know that Yahweh is enough

And sometimes even now, when I don't know how
To get along in this crazy old world
I make a mistake and, by doubt, separate
Myself from the glory Yahweh's unfurled

But I hate the lies, the confusion in my mind
That which keeps the Promise from manifesting
I want everyone to know and be able to show
The love of Father Yahweh that He's blessing

But if I rise up and see the Truth that's redeemed,
Look at things from a different perspective,
I'll remember what's real and what Yahweh's revealed;
The underlying Truth is still protected

Though I still don't understand, and sometimes I get mad,
I will cling to Truth that is unchanging
Even if I don't know, that means nothing. I know
Yahweh's purpose and plan He is arranging

So by faith I'll believe, remember, and receive
The Promise of the Father that He's spoken
Though confusion still hurts, Yahweh's overcome the curse
Underneath the lies, the light is still unbroken.

Remember

Puzzle Pieces

Growing up, gaining perspective
Remembering the Promise
Organizing puzzle pieces
Knowing our original purpose

The framework for creation
That Yahweh set in place,
Yahweh's revelation
Order of time and space

Putting it all together
In the framework in our mind
Seeing the whole picture
Of Yahweh's grand design

Revelation's order,
Purpose manifest
Yahweh shows us His framework
When we give our first and best

Maturity doesn't just happen
Unless we choose to press in
We grow up when we start to see
Yahweh's original vision

The Promise that He made us
The purpose of our lives
Each revelation a puzzle piece
Of the big picture of Christ

Prophetically we receive
The puzzle's individual pieces
Then apostolically we see
What framework is needed

Submitting to the order
Of Yahweh's grand design
We manifest our facet
Of the anointing of the Christ.

Remember

The Way

The Way of Righteousness is strong
Steady, certain, and unchanging above the circles of the Earth
It cannot be broken, cannot be altered
It is there
For us
Not to condemn or repel us when we don't do right
But gently leading and inviting us
Home
He has been there all along
Waiting
And He will wait until no more waiting can be done
Listen,
And you shall hear Him calling,
A gentle voice in your spirit,
A whisper on the wind.

Leading of the Way

The path of righteousness is open
The Way is now unblocked
It's waiting there inside of you
The door has been unlocked

He leads me in the righteous paths
He gives me now His Way
He takes me on to gloriousness
He walks with me each day

He does not call me onward
As His faithful, holy son
And then leave me by myself,
Rather, He leads us with our young

For He gave us each a vision
Over which to steward and grow
He unlocked all the potential
When He allowed us again to know

He teaches us His Promise
Without anger or frustration
He gently leads us forward
To our coming jubilation

He knew when He created us
That we would have our doubts
He wanted to relate to us
So He laid the Way on out

The Way came down to lead us home
He gave Himself for our lives
He will never leave us alone
He wants us to grow and thrive

And the Way leads forward, onward
We shall stand over the conquered
The Holy Promises, unshaken Word
Echoes of Heaven, Way remembered.

Revitalizing the Garden of Eden

I have not destroyed the Garden of Eden
For I have preserved it in you
I give it here now,
You take it in freedom
For you've willingly laid your life down

Once only safe when hidden
It's time to be revealed
For there are now other protections
That I've established for My zeal

It's time to reveal the Promise
I'm calling you forth and out
I'm promising My vision,
What I first spoke aloud

There is a Promise now of Eden
For My people, the Promise remains
For I placed it *in* you, My people
Reveal it now by faith

When you manifest the Promise
Trust in what I say
I have given you protection
I will keep My Promise safe.

I'm making new the Garden
Revitalizing the seed
But just as the first time I spoke it
It takes time to be fully seen

I'm shining the light in your heart
In worship, I nourish your soil
For here I have planted the Garden
That it bring forth fruit in your soul.

Promise Keeper

The perfect work that I have done
I have already completed
Every battle I have won
Every enemy defeated

Take your place in Victory's courts
In splendor be arrayed
Know the Truth that I purport
The plan that I have made

Stand tall in the lion's den
Do not quake before Goliath
Remember who you've always been
And raise your head in triumph

When you walk on darkened paths
Remember the light inside
Darkness surely never lasts
So let My Glory shine

Remember what I've promised you
What I wove into your being
Worship in Spirit and in Truth
Allow yourself to see

Walk upon a higher path,
Listen to a higher Way
Don't be distracted by the task
Abandon what you use to think

Know what you've never known before
Yet what's always been part of you
Take a step through Heaven's door
Know that your Father loves you

Return to the place where you were made
The Ocean of Creation
You're still surrounded by My Promises
They just have a different manifestation

All that I needed to create,
My Promise and My Faith,
I placed these deep inside of you,
They're still in the world today

Hope and purpose, Promised Truth
Peace and joy and love
All that was spoken into you
Will always be enough

The Promise that's inside of you
Woven into your essence
Is reignited and is fueled
When you come into My presence

So come and worship, dance with Me!
Step into your Promise
I am holding out the key
And I will keep you honest

I am the God who purifies
I'm zealous for My Promise
I hid it just to keep it safe
In you I've made it a place of honor

I spoke a Promise to your heart
Then built safety around it
This is truly who you are
You are Heaven's Promise

Promise and keeper safe in one
I made you with this power
I sent you out so I could come
You help Me keep My Promise

This is the reason I have made you
You are my Promised Provision
Remembering when I created you
You are able to live it.

Remember

Apostolic Promise

Before there was time and before there was space
There was only my Father Yahweh
He lived and He moved and He was all there is
But He wanted an expression that would be His

So He created all good and glorious things
He did so just by speaking
He set forth a Word, a Promise He made
Such a marvelous undertaking

All of creation was formless and void
But Yahweh was very excited
For He would bring order to cacophonous noise
He would regulate what He ignited

Let there be Light! Yahweh called aloud
And, brilliantly, light was shone
He saw it was good, and He was very proud
His glory could now become known

He spoke into being all that ever will be
He gave each creation a purpose
And as He kept speaking the Great Tapestry
Yahweh put in order His Promise

This is how it is, this is how it should be,
This is the order I've given,
This order must be part of all living things,
That's part of the Promised Provision

And so the great chaos, the clambering noise
The cacophony of what Yahweh'd spoken
Was brought into order, was given some poise
Was made to be whole and unbroken

We are His Promise, but we must align
We must submit to Yahweh's Lordship
For it was His purpose, it was His design
By doing so, we give Him worship.

Remember

For the King

Once upon a time
There was a great and glorious King
He knew He was so good and so glorious
That He decided He should give Himself a present

So He took it upon Himself to create a new work
Such as had never been seen before
Or since. He guided Himself by His own Words
As He made the work of His hand
And in the end, He saw that it was good
And He was very pleased with the gift He had made for Himself.

The gift was marvelous, for the King had given it life
His very breath He breathed in it
And it moved to the rhythm of His heart.
His heart throbbed with pleasure in the gift that He had made for Himself.

He gave it autonomy, for He was such a great Giver
That He could not make a gift that would only please Himself
He also decided to give gifts to the gift,
And He gave gifts to men
So that everyone could partake in the gift that He had made for Himself.

Now the gift could keep on giving, for in autonomy,
The gift could be a triple portion blessing gift
Given once by the King to Himself,
And again to the gift
Now it could also be given again by the gift to the King
And I am very blessed to be a part of the gift that He had made for Himself.

Each day, we choose to be a gift,
A gift for our King
For we know it's a great blessing to be able to give Him
Anything. After all that He has given us, we want to give to Him
And so we thrill in pleasure
That we can give back the gift that He had made for Himself.

It is a constant, conscious choice
To live for the King
To lay our lives down at His feet
And forever, well and truly be
A gift of Yahweh's pleasure, a gift that He has made for Himself.

Remember

Edge

I
Am always
Living on the edge
But it is not the fun, thrilling
Adventure that it should be

Instead, I balance precariously
On the line between fear and faith
Even when I know better,
Know better than to be afraid

I feel like life is one giant tightrope walk
One mistake could send you downward
Spiraling toward your doom

One mistake and I could be fired
One mistake and I could lose someone
One mistake and everything falls apart
One thread pulled, and the whole tapestry unravels

What nonsense!
What pure, utter nonsense!

There is no safety in Babylon
Every day is a risk,
Every moment could be a killer
Nobody is trustworthy
And nothing is sure
Everything you've worked for could fall apart in an instant
Nothing is constant

That is why we cannot put our faith in Babylon
We cannot build on an unsteady foundation
We cannot put our lives in the hands of something that is ultimately
Crumbling

Instead, we must remember,
Remember the Promise of the Father
Which is sure, steady, unshaken
Immutable, and not subject to change

It is far more certain a path that we can walk on
For it is not based on what we do,
Our successes or mistakes
It is based only on Yahweh and His Word

His passion and zeal will perform this
His passion and zeal will accomplish this
His passion and zeal…
Not me,
Not my effort and strife
Not my passion and zeal
Not my wanting it beyond anything else
Just Him

Just Yahweh and His sure, steady Word
His Promise
His Power
He can do this!
His completely fulfilled Word
That lives in me
That keeps me safe
That brought me back to Him as He came back for me
He loves me
That love is steady

I will have faith in that love
And balance on the edge
Because nothing can hurt me when Yahweh is for me
The edge cannot be scary
When there is no doom to fall to
Because Yahweh's Promise is the safety net

I just need the eyes to see it.

Remember

Demonstrative Faith

The faith that we have beforehand
Is a witness of the faithfulness of Yahweh
Confirmed by the subsequent manifestation
Of all that He Promised in the Beginning.

Remember

Witness

I have walked a million miles
To have the wonder of a child
To see the Promise of a Holy God

Whatever I have to walk through
The path of glory I will choose
For no matter what, I know He's worth it all

Of Yahweh's Promise I have glimpsed
I know that I was made for this!
So I will count it worthy all the cost

I will set my face like flint
And evermore I will press in
So the Promise of the Father shan't be lost

Pressing on and pressing through,
I will walk in Yahweh's Truth
It's then that I will truly start to see

I will remember and I'll know
Then Yahweh's Glory I shall show
And I will have the confidence to be

I am Yahweh's Glory in the Earth
His embodied redemption from the curse
The weight and value of Yahweh's design

All that He planned and then created
When He established manifestation
Eternity then visible in time

Yahweh's Power coursing through me
It will uplift and not undo me
That Yahweh's Will become the essence of the Earth

For once I've seen the Father's heart
His Glory I can now impart
And once and for all shatter any curse.

Remember

Identify with Christ

By faith crucified, by faith chose to die
By faith and Holy Spirit resurrected
By faith lived the life of Yahweh's own Christ
By faith embodied truth and right perspective

By faith identified, by faith glorified
By faith imbued with the power of God
By faith, truth, and love, Word and Spirit were enough
By faith the victory was surely won

By faith demonstrated, by faith contemplated
By faith renewed determination's might
For by faith was reminded to have faith in the night
And by faith bring back the Holy One's pure light

By faith, Word was spoken, by faith still unbroken
By faith and righteousness from God on High
By faith, truth and purpose revealed through real worship
By faith all was redeemed and set to right

By faith shared with others, by faith became brothers
By faith the Kingdom of Heaven came to dwell
By faith in the Earth, by faith ended the curse
By faith received His Lordship in themselves

By faith we are Christ and like Yahshua lay down our lives
To by faith become all we were meant to be
By faith take a stand upheld by Yahweh's right hand
And help Him to come and set creation free.

The Promise is Mine to Keep

I will do whatever it takes
To keep the Promise that I made
The Word I spoke long before time
The righteousness of My design

For I so loved the world I made
I sent My Promise out again
A Word, a Son, Only Begotten
That the world remember what it'd forgotten

Zealously I keep My Promise
I came back to set it free
Ever-growing My metron is
Never ending is the increase

First, I remind you of the Promise
It grows in the greenhouse of your soul
Then, I expose your full-grown harvest
That the world again can know

Know that I have kept My Promise
Know that now I keep it still
Know that I am always honest
Know that I will never fail

Steady on, I am unchanging
Fulfilling all My spoken Word
When this Truth you are engaging,
You shall see what you have heard

I have come to keep My Promise
And I keep it now in you
Rest and trust in all I've promised
Be at peace, for I am true.

Flourish

Sitting on the edge of the Garden of Eden
Knowing that it's time to enter in
Watching all the trees bear fruit and flowers bloom
I rejoice in what I will have again

Only by faith can I traverse the Garden's boundary line
Only by faith of fruit can I partake
But that does not negate the difficulties of a life
Lived to bring Heaven to the Earth by grace

Trusting in the Father's plan, that He has made a way
Believing in the Father's hidden purpose
Walking in the full anointing given by Yahweh
Knowing that there's nothing to reverse it

Pressing forward, moving on, growing toward the Father
Who knew that we the Garden imitate?
We also grow into the light and bloom just like a flower
When nourished by our Holy Spirit's grace

So I will take my place now in the center of my Eden
Flourishing here in my Promised soil
I will rest now in the hands of Him who has completed
All He started, finished without toil.

Remember

Living Echoes

The sound of Yahweh's spoken Word echoing throughout time
Resonating gently into space
Vibrations manifesting a great purpose and design,
An order that the Holy Word dictates

For those that have the ears to hear become a living echo
Repeating what we've heard through all creation
We will have the faith to bear the Promise of the Father
And find our kin in every tribe and nation

Holding now My Father's heart, the greatest gift and blessing
A demonstration so the world can know
The purpose and the peace that comes from the Father's lordship
And all the glory that His Truth can show

Vibrating and resonating with the heartbeat of the Father
As His Word causes our own hearts to beat
By faith we echo back His Word and it is heard so clearly
Confirmation makes His Promises complete.

Empowered

Reigniting the light that You placed inside our hearts
As we draw closer to the flame
Like a camel in the desert to which you impart
Refreshing water of life as we worship Your Name

I've come from the desert to draw near to You
My Holy and filling oasis
I recognize that Your Voice is all that is true
As I am abiding in Your infinite places

You strengthen me as I imbibe Holy Power
Then I can accomplish Your goal
Redeeming the purpose in Your lost creation
For You've come to make it all whole

The hope of creation for which it's long cried
That we as Your sons take our places
We are Your Promise, for You've sent us out
But we only are as You have graced us

The drumming of the Father's heart beats in our breasts
The sure knowing inside does sustain us
For we bring our Father the first and the best
In worship, He comes to reclaim us

We burst forth like lightning from our Father's presence
Empowered, by Yahweh's own Promise
We can do anything if we believe
And when Holy Spirit enthralls us

Nothing can stop us when He sends us out
Burning with an everlasting flame
The strength of omnipotence from the gentle touch
Of Yahweh, my Father's, embrace.

Perform

We are well able to perform what Yahweh promised
For we are empowered by Christ
We have been baptized in Yahweh's anointing
He gives us the grace for our lives

Taking the victory Yahweh has given
Becoming the Promise of God
So even in failure we will be winning
For this is redemption full-on

From Yahweh's perspective, there's no disappointment
There's no condemnation or loss
Remember, as carriers of Christ's anointing,
Sometimes we must go to the cross

So Yahweh is able to accomplish His blessing
And fulfill the Promise through us
For if we are pure of heart, we'll let Yahweh change us
His Word and His Spirit, enough

He will restore all that we have broken
He makes us whole and redeemed
But it's through our choices that Yahweh has spoken
As we lay it all at His feet

Faithfully waiting to fulfill the Promise
Manifested anointing of God
Sometimes the journey doesn't seem like it's righteous
To us, it can look rather odd

But Yahweh's responsible to keep His Promise
He'll keep it no matter what
For He has been waiting for those who will trust Him
Who come into agreement with His love

A pure heart is all He needs for His own purpose
For He brings the power Himself
Even in trouble, then, we can still worship
For in Him, in Yahweh, all's well

Repentance brings victory, gives Yahweh access
Allows Him to work once again
In every circumstance and situation
It is by this process we win.

Bread and Wine

The bread and wine are the Promise
The spoils of war our old lives
We trade who we once were to Yahweh
By choosing to give Him a tithe

In return we receive both the Covenant
And the Power to make it our own
For only by Word and by Spirit
Can the Father's full Promise be shown

The choosing's so very important
For we need more than just to see
To make manifest Yahweh's vision
We must become His Zadokim

Zadokim are the ones who have chosen
To be priests of Yahweh Most High
To minister to Him our offering:
The entire expanse of our lives

Then we shall be a Holy Nation
A bevy of Yahweh's righteous sons
And we shall become revelation
To the world of what Yahweh has done

In ministering to the Father
We represent Him to the world
In being His priests, we then become kings
The Promise of Glory revealed.

R e m e m b e r

Friendship

When you remind me of Yahweh's Promise
That He made to me before time
And I do the same for you.

Unbreakable Promise

It is Yahweh's job
To keep His Promise
It is His passion and zeal
It is for this reason
His Son died
It is for this reason
I am alive
It is Yahweh's purpose
To keep His Promise

It is my job
To submit to His Promise
To let Him redeem
What He wants to see
To allow Him to show
His glory through me
That all the world know
And come to be
It is my gift
Not to break the unbreakable Promise

If I've clean hands
And a heart that's pure
Then I cannot lose
Victory is sure
Because I will choose
To let Yahweh in
Allow Him to do
What He already did
I will not break the unbreakable Promise
Yahweh keeps His unbreakable Promise.

Remember

Sovereignty

That nothing can ever dethrone Yahweh
Or cause His will
Not to be done
In its entirety
In the Earth.

Chosen Generation

We are His
A chosen generation
A royal priesthood
A holy convocation

We submit
To the government of Promise
To the Word of Yahweh's order
To the blessings of the Father

We will live
To walk out Yahweh's purpose
To see manifestation
To know that He is worth it

We're most blessed
To be given this assignment
To be brought into His presence
To be offered bread and wine

We've chosen
To be Yahweh's presentation
Of all that He has Promised
To every generation.

Remember

Drowning

Once again,
I feel like I am drowning
But it's okay this time
I've learned to breathe underwater.

Overwhelming

Sometimes
I think it's just too much
Yahweh is overwhelming
Overwhelmingly good
Overwhelmingly zealous
Overwhelmingly deep
Overwhelmingly expansive
Overwhelmingly, exhaustingly God
And He has blessed us with the ability to know Him
And I have always desired to know Him
Overwhelmingly
But if I saw Him in His overwhelming entirety
I would be utterly overwhelmed!
So He has blessed us with the process
That leads us to know Him more and more
A little at a time
So as not to be so overwhelming.

Remember

The Fire's Story

Once upon a time in a Kingdom far away
There lived a giant fire, an overwhelming flame
The flame did burn so brightly, the flame did burn so hot
For that is fire's nature; there is no way it could not

So the fire burned so brightly, but the fire was alone
For who could withstand the heat that came from the fire's throne
There was no other element could come near to the fire
And any time it tried to, it risked its very life

The wood was burned to ashes, the rocks forever scorched
The water evaporated, yes, everything was torched
But the fire wanted relationship, for nothing should be alone
But only at a distance could the fire be somewhat known

Then one day the fire had a great revelation
It set a plan in motion that gave it great jubilation
The fire was so joyful, for the fire realized
That fire can only be completely known by other fire

So it sent out an invitation to all who wanted to come
To every single nation and every single tongue
All the elements on Earth eventually to the fire came
But they would not be burned if they accepted fire's flame

There were some elements that always longed to know the fire
Inside of them was burning a bright and true desire
When to them the invitation came, they quickly did accept
The fire sent them His own flame, He gave to them Himself

The elements would have to change, would have to become fire
But that was just the only way to receive their heart's desire
So we took the flame inside ourselves the fire so to be
And in doing so we became capable of approaching the fire in peace

The fire burned more brightly as its flames to it returned
Together we shall cause the whole entire world to burn
But the burning is not destructive, the burning is just right
For without the flame of fire, we would forever lack the light

As all flames return to the fire, the fire itself does grow
Until it covers all the Earth and is well and truly known
The desire of the fire's heart was now forever sated
For the fire would be known by all that from fire was created

The fire has relationship, what it wanted from the start
And all the other elements have the desires of their hearts
For to come to know the fire is the greatest gift of life
But in order to live in fire, first we must learn how to die

The fire, the burning had to come; it is the only way
But happily it did not come at once, it first sent out its flames
The flames prepare the fire's path, fulfills fiery desire
So that instead of receiving fiery wrath, we are completed in the fire.

Remember

Origin

I originate
In a place
Where right and wrong do not exist
In that place was Yahweh, me,
And all that ever truly is
There was no right
There was no wrong
For how could there ever have been?
Right can only counter wrong
And Yahweh makes no wrong
As long as I
Remain true
To who I was in the origin-place
I can confidently say
I cannot make a mistake
I cannot receive rejection
People have no right to judge
I will walk in manifestation
Of all that ever truly was
For all that is
Is all Yahweh said
Everything else
Doesn't really exist
So I'll be true to original me
Of right and wrong, I am forever free.

Remember

The Way Back Home

There's a long, long road
That will lead me home
With many valleys
And mountains

I walk it day by day
Full of anointed faith
Sometimes it's the only thing
That keeps me going

But I am not left alone
My Father's walking me home
Seeing me to the door
To His heart

And I was made for this
Purposed to rest in Him
And to enjoy the journey
Though it's long

I have dreamt a thousand dreams
To see what I was meant to see
For I have walked a thousand miles
From home

And I will take a thousand breaths
To return to the place that I had left
And I will find the place
Where I belong

The path was laid out for me
From the very beginning
And I can choose to stay
Or walk away

The road is long and hard
But the Promise is just too good
To choose anything else
At the end of the day

So I will stay on this road
It's the only road leading home
And I know only on this road
Am I safe

And I will dream so many dreams
And see what I was meant to see
For I will choose to take every step
Back home

I know that Yahweh's resolute
So I will set my face too
Together we shall find
The Way back home
To the place where I belong.

Fearless

My breath comes in short gasps
And my heart, it pounds again
I cannot see how I can do the task
Win all I'm asked to win

I start to feel very alone
And like nobody wants me
Like I will never have a home
Unless I do all things perfectly

I wonder when I shall see
The fearlessness Yahweh promised me
When I shall be able to live my life
Without constant fear of dying inside

Sometimes I wonder what is life
I know it's more than fear and strife
I know You've promised better things
Given me freedom from all fear brings

Yet I still fight, labor, and toil
For I'm afraid that if I fail
I shall forever be abandoned
By all who claim to love me well

Yet Promises are greater than fear
And I know the Truth within
So even though I may not feel it
I know I always win

And I am not a slave to fear
For Yahweh's called me, brought me here
He takes my hand and leads me in
To places where I've longed to go

But I must choose to take my place
And let no fear or doubt remain
Remembering victory's reign
And the certainty of home

That nothing that I ever do
Can call me, now, away from You
Your Word, Yahweh, forever true
Will lead me, guide me home to You.

Nothing Can Stop the Kingdom

Carrying the Kingdom
Into every situation
Protected deep inside of us
As we enter tribes and nations

Encapsulated in a Word
That is a Holy Promise
Yahweh, Your Kingdom will be heard
In every heart that's honest

The sovereignty of Yahweh
Is total and absolute
Nothing can stop the Kingdom
So I stand resolute

Firm on the foundation
Of the Apostles and the Prophets
We build a Holy Nation
That shall embrace the Promise

Today if I embrace the Word
I will receive the Promise
Resting in what I have heard
Knowing victory's upon us

Every tribe and tongue and nation
Shall somehow be redeemed
And the glory shall be much greater
For how impossible it seems

Trusting You to rule
Trusting You to reign
We now return our lives to You
As we worship You today

Dwelling in Your Presence
I share My Father's heart
I am in full assurance
Of everything You are

I know if You have authored it
You will now come and perfect
Nothing can ever stop your will
To dead things resurrect

Such joy is set before You
For all that You have done
Everything that shall ever be
You have already won.

The Place Where We Belong

We are born as strangers
Strangers in a strange land
On a journey back home
To the place where we belong

As babies, we cry out in confusion
Confusion at the strange land
And how it is not our home,
The place where we belong

As we grow, we think we learn
And we acclimate to the strange land
And we begin to think it is our home
The place where we belong

There is always a part inside
A part that longs for and cries
A part that knows this is a strange land
Not the place where we belong

If we listen to that voice,
The part inside that gives us vision
We can return from this strange land
To the place where we belong

For the voice belongs to our Creator,
Our Father, the one true Revelator
He tells us how to leave this strange land
And brings us back to the place where we belong

Once we're home, we see things clearly
We can see the longing cries
Groans that come from the strange land
Wanting also to return to the place where it belongs

So we sojourn in creation
To redeem our apportioned lot
That the strange land might also come
Home to the place where it belongs

For the Father promised redemption
For every tribe and tongue and nation
Every single ecosystem, all the land and flora and fauna
He has given us a place where we belong

I take my place, gladly writing
My spirit man inside exciting
To remind us all so we won't be strangers
To the place where we belong.

Wise Eyes

Eyes that see the truth in people
That see the bigger picture
That survey circumstances
And know who is the victor

Eyes that know what Yahweh knows
Have seen what Yahweh's seen
Eyes that trust that where they go
Leads to fulfilled dreams

Eyes that choose to take a risk
With Yahweh to align
Eyes that look at the heart of man
These are the Eyes of Christ.

Remember

If I Could Just Remember

If I could just remember
The love You had for me
When You spoke me into being
The Promise that You made me
Before You sent me out into time and space

If I could just remember
The relationship we had
When I knew without any question
Your character, Your faithfulness
That You were a Father to me
Created me in love
And wanted only the best for me

If I could just remember
Who You created me to be
And that all that I need to be
Is me
And there is nothing I could do
Or not do
To change the fact that You love me,
Want only good for me,
There is nothing I can do
To stop Your Promises from coming true

If only I could remember
Your Word, Your Will, Your Truth
Then I would not have to dig around
In the dirt of doubt
And be buried by questions You've already answered
I would never go down
That rabbit trail of "what if" and fear

If I could remember,
Then I would remember
That the enemy is powerless,
A toothless lion,
A defanged snake,
An illusion created by imperception
Nothing,
And his only hope is to make me forget
That he has no power
And I have everything
Because I am Your child,
The child of the King

But I choose to remember
Even though it is still just
Fuzzy in my mind
I will remember!
I will see the Christ inside!
And know that
I am powerful,
I have Promises
I am purposed to be here
And now
Because I will remember
And I will be a reminder to all the world
So that the enemy will tremble to hear
My very name

I am the Rememberer.
I am the Promise.
I will not forget.

Remember

Time to Engage

I come into Your Presence
To listen to Your heart
I learn who I am
I receive who You are

The time of dying is over
It's time to come alive
To manifest the power
That You've placed here inside

Boldly moving forward
Bringing Heaven to the Earth
Carrying on Your Word
Giving purpose birth

Flowing in Your Spirit
I have Your heart and mind
I'll be Your Word so all can hear it
I present to all the Christ

Coming into agreement
With the Word You speak to me
Just by receiving Your completion
I have come to be

Once I am, it's time for action
It is time to demonstrate
Set your face and gain some traction
Force the world to engage

All the universe's power
Residing here inside
The world will have to reckon
With this manifested Christ

Just be faithful and be fearless
There's a dynamo inside
The world will have to hear it
And then have to decide

Complete in who I am
But more complete together
We present an option
For all to choose the better

For when all come to completion
In the unity of Christ
We bring our Father pleasure
As He receives the prize

All that He saw from the Beginning
And purposed so to be
We shall have a part in fulfilling
Just by choosing to be free.

Remember

Rise Up

Rise up and see the Promise
That I made to you, My Son
I will not allow it to be lost
I will again make all things one

Walk in the completion
Walk in the finished work
When you do so, you remind them
Of My Holy Word

Rise up and see the vision
That I purposed before time
Rise up and *be* the vision
That I called you forth to shine

Rise up and be the person
That I spoke you now to be
Rise up and know the Word that
I continue now to speak

I called you out in purpose
I've given you a place
You have a reason for being here
That you should embrace

I've given you all power
To be what I called you out for
Stand up and take your places
Grow up, I've called you forth!

Arise! Arise! My children
Have become My mighty sons
An army of the righteous
A host of the first Heaven

Leave back all temerity
Leave behind all fear
I've dealt in all severity
With any enemy that's here

Walk in the Promised victory
Show all what I can do
Reveal to the world the mystery
That I have placed in you

Be My demonstration
In the Heavens and the Earth
You've been tested and you've triumphed
It's time for you to birth

It is such a giant calling
But I've given it to you
Because I know that I can trust you
To stay forever true

Rise up and trust My Power
Rise up and trust in Me
Rise up and trust yourself
Rise up now and be.

Remember

Held

I was made to hold You
And be held by You
To be completely surrounded
By Your Spirit and Your Truth

I was made a Promise
That will never be moved
That You will never stop
Holding me in You

I was made important
For I hold a Holy God
He lives inside me always
Together we are One

As I walk in creation
He walks in it as well
And all the tribes and nations
Can choose in Him to dwell

Each of us is a facet
Of our Holy God
If we choose to express Him
The world can see His love

Only my expression
Can reach a certain part
Only your expression
Can fulfill Yahweh's heart

The glory of the Father
Will only be complete
When all embrace the part of Him
That they embody

Thank You, Holy Spirit
That You came in me to live
That You offered me a purpose
That Your Promise I can give.

Remember

The Power of Love

I have the power
To overcome all that tries to come against me
Because Yahweh loved me enough
To give me the power
When I was still powerless

I have the power
To overcome all that tempts and torments me
Because Yahshua loved me enough
To die for me to have this power
When I did not even know Him

I have the power
To overcome all that tries to keep me from fulfilling my purpose
And receiving the fullness of my Promise
Because Holy Spirit loves me
And is in me today
He is this power
And I am no longer powerless.

Remember

On Repentance for Doubting

I doubted You loved me, I doubted You cared
I doubted You'd save me from all that's out there
I doubted You'd heal me, that You'd bring me home
I doubted You wanted to call me Your own

I doubted Your freedom, I doubted Your Word
I doubted You'd listen, I doubted what I heard
I doubted My Father had it all figured out
But now I repent of such sorrowful doubt

I remembered the Promise, remembered Your love
Now I remember that You are enough
You are faithful to do what You said that you would
You honor Your Promise as only You could

You've given me blessings, You've given me joy
You've kept every Word that it not return void
You're trustworthy in all things, sovereign and true
Everything's finished when it is in You

So I'm sorry for doubting, there's never a need
For You are the One who's made all things complete
Whatever may happen, no matter what
I am Yours and You're mine and that is enough.

R e m e m b e r

Safe

That there is nothing
That can take me from You
Nothing that can stop
Your Word from coming true

There is nothing
That can dethrone my King
Nothing that can stop Him
From ruling and reigning

That there is nothing
That can stop me now
For I've remembered Yahweh
And that He's given me the power

There is nothing
That can stop my God
For He is sovereign Creator,
Ruler of all that ever was

There is nothing
That can stop His Word
For in every single spirit
His Word shall soon be heard

There is nothing
That can hurt me now
For I am in the arms of Yahweh
And He keeps me safe and sound.

Remember

The Things I Cannot Show You

I have so much more to show you
Than the things you've seen before
Such glory and such purpose
I have for you in store

Such beauty and such splendor
Your life will be to Me
But for now it's only hoped for,
A whisper in a dream

Before I let you see it,
I must mold you into shape
For the character to receive it
Is preeminent

If I had shown you beforehand
What you're walking in right now
You would've tried to make it happen
Or else killed it with doubts

Instead I give you glimpses
So you can look forward to
Everything your heart desires,
Which you'll have when all is through

It's a hope that keeps you going
Through the dark and trying times
But it's only a small portion
Of what I have for you in Christ

Though I know you are frustrated
At what's just beyond your reach
Know I keep it for you for a reason
And one day you'll fully see

Oh the things I cannot show you
Are amazing to behold
But you know this already
For you've received a hundredfold

Looking back at what your life's been
Could you ever have imagined
The glory that you live in
Deeper than you could've fathomed

Then look forward and imagine
What I will one day give to you
Greater even than things hoped for
But assured to be true.

R e m e m b e r

Gifts & Graces

Gifts and graces are tools
Used to express Yahweh in the Earth
They allow the finite to contemplate
The Infinite
They become a demonstration
Of the Father's Heart
They are beautiful,
But they cannot get in the way

I have the gift of poetry,
Of expressing the Father in words
Of taking His infinite revelation
And putting it into parables
It is beautiful, flowing in your gift
Operating in your grace
Reading the words on a page
That only exist because you said, "Yes"
When Yahweh asked you to put them there
And I take nothing away from gifts and graces
When I say

At the end of the day
It's all about Yahweh
Relating to Him and the beauty
That He is
A grace is only good if it brings you closer to Him

At the end of the day,
He loves me
And we relate together
In the cool of the day
Beautiful!

Purposed grace, you remind us of this
And we remember
At the end of the poem
He loves us.

Queen of Eden

Walking unafraid in the Garden of Eden
Surveying all that was bequeathed to me
Living out my days in love and true freedom
Abiding with my Father, full, complete

Knowing why I'm here and all I was made for
Seeing all there ever was to see
Administering faithfully Yahweh's creation
All wound up in who I'm called to be

Though we saw a fall, there is redemption
An underlying truth of all there is
Knowing through it all, the Promise of Yahweh
Remains, abiding joy, we're always His

I am still a Queen in the Garden of Eden
I have still been called to rule and reign
I still have the power that Yahweh has given
This is still my uncontested domain

So I will walk unafraid in my Kingdom
Knowing it's really Yahweh's Kingdom still
For I will not remain confused by a snake's tongue
Redemption says that all is good and well.

Remember

The Knowledge of Christ

The knowledge of Christ
A superseding stream
Nothing can stand against it
It's the victory received

For what good is the power
That's hidden deep inside
If we don't know we have it
And can't bring it to light

It is our greatest weapon
The knowledge of this power
And that we have access to it
In every needful hour

When we've knowledge of omnipotence
The Christ that dwells in us
We can release the evidence
For what faith makes substance of

Not only that we have it
But that power we can wield
When we submit to Yahweh
And to Holy Spirit yield

The sword of Yahweh's power
The weapon of His Word
The knowledge that we have it
Is victory assured

Walking in the knowledge
That only comes from Christ
Is such an honored privilege
And as sons, it is our right

Stand tall and take your places
My holy, righteous sons
Know all that is inside you
And that you've already won.

Remember

The Beauty of Omnipotence (The Worship of the Mind)

Oh, Yahweh our omnipotence,
The source of all true power
To You I willingly submit
That my mind You can scour

But I can't walk in power
Until I give my mind to You
I can't display You in the Earth
Until I submit to Truth

So work Your power in my mind
Tear down all that is old
Rebuild me with the mind of Christ
Make me courageous and bold

Wipe me clean of all that's false
As I set my mind on You
Then I receive omnipotence
Because Your Word is the Truth

Build a city on a hill
A light that's shining bright
But all that starts when I am still
And worship You with my mind

My mind becomes a place of peace
A place I can express
The glory of the Christ in me
As I give You the first and best

Worship is a mindset
Established now in me
It has removed the blinders
So that I have eyes to see

The beauty of omnipotence
That's flowing out of me
But only after it has cleansed
The mind inside of me

The beauty of omnipotence
Beyond all right and wrong
The glory that we will express
As we sing Yahweh's song

Our lives then become worship
A living, prayerful song
When we trust in Yahweh's purpose
That we've had all along

Fearing not what we'll look like
When we lose all control
When we're called to express the Christ
As He has made us whole.

Remember

Returning to the Garden

Eve, the mother of women,
And also the mother of men
The first one to believe a lie
The first person to sin

Adam, the father of nations
Ruler of all of the Earth
The first one to abandon his place
The first one to inhabit a curse

They had all the power of Heaven
They operated in the creation
Then there was a lie that was spoken
And Satan inherited the nations

Then Yahshua came, second Adam
And for us He died on the cross
He was the Way back to the Garden
Saving all from becoming lost

We can return to the Garden
But the snake speaks to us every day
He tells us Yahweh doesn't love us
He says that there isn't a Way

But when the snake says we're not worthy
That there's something horribly wrong
Instead of eating from his tree
We can tell the snake to be gone

Thereby we return to the Garden
Only this time there won't be a fall
When we tell the snake we believe Him
Who made us and gave us His all

Then we do not eat of the fruit
That comes from the lies of the snake
The Tree of Knowledge loses its power
When we decide not to partake

I am still Queen of the Garden
I eat of the Tree of Life
I rule and reign in the Earth
I know that Yahweh is mine

I banish the snake from the Garden
By believing that all is quite well
Whispers of the snake cannot harm me
When I forget all the lies that he tells.

Remember

Be Gone!

Once again, I am presented
With the old eternal choice
To believe the Truth inherent
Or listen to a false voice

Here I stand by Trees of Knowledge
Right beside the Tree of Life
A snake calls and beckons to me
He wants me to believe a lie

But I have been here before
I recognize this spot
I won't submit to him to tries
To tell me what I'm not

I have Christ's wisdom and Christ's power
I am onto evil's ways
So I will stand and say, "Be gone now!"
And laugh in the enemy's face

I will take the Truth upon me
I will be a Tree of Life
It's planted deep inside my heart
I just have to recognize

I will remember who I am
I am Queen here in this place
The enemy cannot take from me
What I have retained by faith

It doesn't matter what he says
The words he speaks are always lies
So I reject him fully, outright
And eat from the Tree of Life

Once I've partaken of this glory
That My Father's shared with me
I can rise up with the victory
And totally reign as Queen

Queen of Eden, Queen of Heaven
For I am the Bride of Christ
He's redeemed me, Oh! Redemption!
Oh the glorious Tree of Life!

All I am cries HalleluYah
For I remember what I was
Before the snake offered me evil
Saying I was not enough

In my hand I hold a scepter
On my head I wear a crown
Just because this I remember
I can cast the enemy down!

Tools of wisdom, grateful worship
All that Yahweh says is done
I remember His omnipotence
I remember that we're One

Christ the wisdom gives me power
More than knowledge of the lies
Holy Spirit, my Reminder
And He makes me Yahweh's Christ.

Not Perfect

Lead me, oh Father, oh Husband, oh King
Back to all there was in the Beginning
Back to my Home, my Purpose, my Heart
Back to the finish line which is also the start

Back to the place of magnificent power
Where You, I embrace, and find all that You've authored
Back to the Garden where I rule and reign
Only from Your Heart as to You I relate

Oh, Yahweh Father, Yahshua the Way
Holy Spirit the Author of a finished faith
I am Your creation and I am Your Bride
I steward Your Garden as in You I abide

To rest in the Garden, in Your finished work
To abide in the Presence of Your original Word
To hear my own purpose from His very lips
To know I'm not perfect; it's ok, I am His.

Remember
___

Redemption

What were You doing when You came back for me
When You gave up Your life so that I could be free
When You gave up Your Kingdom to die on a cross
When you seemed to lose what could never be lost?

But losing is finding as You surely know
That You made a way for Your Kingdom to grow
Amazing redemption in place from the start
Encoded in the Words You spoke from Your heart

When it looked like it'd fallen, nothing was lost
From the Beginning, You had ordained the cross
Your purposed redemption was already planned
We were never really taken from Your hand

Always and forever, Yours from the start
But only because we exist in Your heart
Reclaimed in redemption, given it all
Because of what You did, there's never a fall

We simply remember all that we are
And You, oh My Father, and what's in Your heart
Sit under the branches of Life's only Tree
Receiving the blessing as we let ourselves be.

Remember

Wisdom is Power

Toss away the human mind
It is a little thing
Receive instead the mind of Christ
And take your place as king

With Yahweh, we can do all things
If we have His heart and mind
Receiving what His Spirit brings
Laying down our lives

Remember all the parts you play
Recall just who you are
Creation's grandeur is displayed
When you take the place that's yours

Yahweh's wisdom is His power
As Holy Spirit knows
We can receive it in this hour
If we listen to all He shows

The whole perspective, little things
And all that's in between
We operate as priests and kings
Revealing mysteries

But human knowledge has no value
And we must let it go
If we're to walk in Yahweh's power
His mysteries to show.

Still I Believe

There are so many things that I want to see
That before, I have never known
There are so many feelings I want to perceive
Things I very much wish was so

But I have not seen what I want to see
It has never before been this way
But when the snake comes and questions me
I'll refute all that he tries to say

Still I believe! I will cry with a shout
In what I've never seen before
Just because inner glory has not yet come out
Doesn't mean it's not waiting in store

Still I believe! It is the Promised Truth
Firmly established before time
It is still there inside all of us who
Have faith to conquer the lies

So yes, I believe! I have faith to inspire
The faith of my Father in me
I will receive all that my heart desires
For Yahweh sets all captives free

I will always believe! Whether or not I've seen
And then faith will give substance to sight
Even when in the darkness nothing's as it seems
I know day always follows the night

And then I will see after I have believed
After I have remembered the Promise
It began in my Father, now it's inside of me
It was from the Beginning accomplished.

Remember

To Operate in Universal Power

I have all the power in the universe
Here inside of me
I have the power to overcome the curse
Yahshua has set me free

But I cannot use the power I have
Unless I remember it's mine
I will not know all that I am
Without choosing to conquer the lies

Sometimes it is hard to remember that
I can operate in universal power
When trials, feelings, and circumstance
Tell me I should just hide and cower

But I will remember when snakes try to talk
When the enemy tells me I'm worthless
Yahshua Himself did not consider it loss
To come redeem me and my purpose

So, I will arise above all hateful lies
And operate in the power I'm given
I will be fine as in faith I abide
And uncover the treasures that're hidden

Yahweh has Promised, He gave me a choice
I can believe Him or falter
But if I decide to obey Yahweh's voice
I will stay in the arms of my Father

Nothing can stop the Promise of God
Unless it is my unbelief
But He's given me the power to overcome
Lies that present themselves to me

So, I overcome with all victory won
Because He has finished the process
It is only that I must believe it is done
To receive the fullness of the Promise.

Renovating the Mind

Come inside the mind of Christ
Let Him now expand it
The renovation of the mind
The blessing that's commanded

Though renovations can be hard,
Knocking down things can be painful
When you find the Word of God
You will know that it is gainful

There are treasures hidden in the walls
Buried under the ground
When condemnations and lies fall
The treasure can be found

So, knock down walls and dig things up
No matter what it costs
Then you'll find unending love
And treasures won't be lost

Though the old must be demolished
To make way for the new
The Word of Yahweh is established
In Spirit and in Truth

In thankfulness, we will be standing
When all is said and done
On sure foundation, firmly planted
A victory that's won

Surrounded by the treasures
That were found inside my mind
Much greater than the pleasures
That would've temporarily been mine

Thank You, Yahweh Father
For the fortitude for renovation
I would trade it for none other
Than to be Your redeemed nation.

Illustrious Illumination

Oh, Illustrious Illumination
You find what's been veiled from our sight
Bringing grand revelation
And hidden things to light

As we're walking out our purpose
We are safe inside Your plan
Whether or not we see it
Or if we understand

Your purpose is not hindered
It's a mighty, rushing flow
But sometimes to take our place
You give us grace to know

Revealing hidden treasures
Revealing hidden Truths
You take Your holy pleasure
When we abide in You

Thank You, Oh Yahweh
Oh, Holy Spirit, dwell
That You will show us the Truth
That all is truly well.

Remember

Christ the Wisdom and the Power

Christ the wisdom for the power
Only when we trust in You
You reveal what You're creating
In Spirit and in Truth

To commune with Holy Spirit
Such a great and glorious gift
For only He can give us access
To all that truly is

You show the heart of Yahweh
You give us the mind of Christ
You are always with us
Oh, that you dwell inside!

To be with You is blessing
Oh! Just to be with You!
It is the greatest of all things
To be able to commune

We forget not what You've Promised
We remember who You are
When on You our eyes are focused
When we have Your whole heart

Oh, to know You for the first time
Is to know You once again
As we have always known You
For the Beginning is the End

We were made just for this knowing
In our minds, the pieces click
Holy Spirit, You're just showing
Us what really, truly is

Holy Spirit, oh the power
For we learn the mind of Christ
As You teach us to remember
What has always been inside

Revelation is the wisdom
That from Holy Spirit comes
The unveiling of perfection
And subsequent transformation!

Then from that revelation
We reveal You to the world
Teaching them to value
That truly priceless pearl

Christ the power for the wisdom
To endure 'til Kingdom comes
When we realize the purpose
And take our place as sons

Oh, the power to believe it
That all that You say is true
On the power to receive it
And to Trust fully in You

Oh, the Promise to creation
Is a Promise to Yourself
That every tribe and nation
Will again come in You to dwell

Oh, the power for completion
"It is finished!" It is done
For You start before You finish
All the battles have been won

Oh, to walk in revelation
And in revelation walk
To believe in full salvation
Never at the process balk

It is finished, You have Promised
We see as we abide in You
For You are always honest
Oh, Holy Spirit of Truth!

Christ is wisdom and is power
Christ lives inside of me
Christ will give in every hour
All that we shall ever need

Relating to revelation
Valuing Him as a son
All His wisdom and His power
That He is the Holy One

Holy Spirit, how I love You!
How I love to take my place
Thank you that I am part of You!
That Your Truth I can embrace!

Vessels

We are the vessels of Eden
We are the vessels of life
We carry in us a secret
We share it with all mankind

We have the Spirit inside us
We can bring Eden to Earth
For when the seed planted is risen
We receive Yahweh's new birth

Growing the Garden from seedlings
But order's important and prime
For before any plant's manifested
We must grow the Tree of Life

Once the Tree of Life's in the center
The rest of the Garden just grows
Nourished by Life's flowing river
Which whispers to the ground so it knows

It will know the seeds deep inside it
It will know how to give them birth
It will know of purpose and order
And all will be free from the curse

All of the Law is established
In Perfection, it's already there
And when touched by Life we remember
To manifest all the Life that we bear

Life opens our eyes to the present
To Yahweh's established, sure ways
Life reminds us that He's sovereign
And in Him all things have been made

He gave us foundational order
Upon which this whole world was created
Though hidden, in these days it's being revealed
To His Apostles and Prophets by faith

We are the vessels of Eden
Made for Holy Spirit to dwell
And as we fully receive Him
We see that all truly is well.

Trust

Faithful creator, Yahweh my God
You finished before You have started
You're a completer, You leave nothing undone
Your Spirit to us You've imparted

Faithfully trusting, we are Your sons
We believe in more than what is seen
Though it doesn't look it, we know all is done
And no other power could ever be

Faithfully waiting, oh manifestation
We walk in creation together
Partnering with Your Spirit, we redeem the nations
For He shows us all back to the Father

Not scorning the process, I know You enjoy
Those who believe in Your Promise
For without the faith that Your sons employ
We will never see what You've shown us

Yahweh, You are faithful, though I did not know
Until Holy Spirit had shown me
But I'll keep believing 'til knowledge is full grown
Because in You all things are complete.

R e m e m b e r

Footsteps

I walk again in the Garden of Eden
Everything my feet touch is under my command
Holy Spirit manifest as I live and breathe Him
Knowing every circumstance is part of Yahweh's plan

Oh, the day is cool and bright, walking with my Father
Oh, the glory we will shine as we receive His Life
Drinking oh so deeply from His ever-flowing River
Everywhere I go all of creation will recognize

The light that shines inside my heart, it emanates from Yahweh
His righteousness I can impart as I abide in Him
All that is and is to come is only what He Promised
For He is all that ever was and in Him only we live

My feet will tread upon the ground as it receives the Promise
I am a faithful steward; over this I rule and reign
Only as I will submit to freedom's Lord and Savior
Never again will I forget what I've received by faith

Remembrance becomes reminder so all creation sees
What Yahweh did Promise in His original plan
Reconnecting with the One who does abide in me
Creation and Creator will then become One again

Original plan trumps original sin, for Yahweh foresaw what He knew
Knowing what would happen,
He gave to us His Spirit and His Truth
And made a way back home for man

Yahshua's last will and testament
Has left some gifts for men
Wisdom and power from His Spirit
Assurance of how it will end

Ending in the Garden from whence it all began
With man ruling again as faithful steward
Relating to Yahweh fully as we've never left His plan
And nothing can stop the power of His True Word.

Remember

Original Plan

All of creation did stretch out before Me
Time and space and all that ever was
Before I ever spoke the Word to set it into motion
I imbued it with a true unyielding Love

I saw the fall, I saw the fear
The loss of my creation
But even before I shed a tear
I had laid out redemption

What Satan meant for evil, I have only meant for good
In all that I created, I wove redemption
So that even from the Beginning, all would be as it should
I made sure it would still be when it ended

In each Word, I placed Myself
I am all that I've spoken
When I said I'd never leave you, I Promised this as well:
You can never be broken.

The Cost

The plan was there inside My mind in glorious completion
Before I spoke a Word to say, "Oh, light, come now to be"
All that was and is and is to come I saw from the Beginning
And I knew every single thing creating would cost Me

Still I chose then to create, I chose to make a Promise
I chose to abide in Love and share it with the world
I chose even then to make a journey to the cross
I knew what it would take to reclaim My priceless pearl

I made you and I loved you even knowing what you'd cost Me
I wanted you, delight in you, even though I knew the price
I never would abandon you, rejecting you's not of Me
I said I would come back for you when I gave you Life

This love is unconditional and you did not surprise Me
When the effects of the fall did manifest in full
Every decision that you made, I reckoned and atoned for
So, receive what I freely give, for I have made you whole

There is no such thing as condemnation when you receive the Promise
The Promise that I made in you when I spoke you into being
The fullness of my love for you is purposed and is glorious
When I look at you I always know it was worth it to Me

I told you once to count the cost before an undertaking
For if you got halfway through and the tower could not be built
How silly and foolish you would look to have ever gotten started
But I would not do such a thing; I knew the price full well

I own the cattle on a thousand hills, I'm the universe's Master
I can afford to pay the price creation has cost Me
I have all the power to save the whole world from disaster
And I do not begrudge the life I gave to set you free

So freely receive what I freely give, let no guilt or condemnation
Stop you from taking on what I hold out now to you
I want you, I want all of you, I take pleasure in your redemption
Gladly I did pay the price to give Myself one like you.

Remember

Unyielding Love

Oh manifestation, oh You love me so
Whatever I do and wherever I go
There's no condemnation for him who's in Christ
Who will willingly choose to give You his life

I am the recipient of unyielding Love
Whatever I do is always enough
I don't have to earn it; it's always been there
Though I don't deserve it, my Father does share.

Remember

At Your Mercy

Into Your hands I commit my life
All I will ever be
All that I have and all desires
I give You willingly

I take my hands now off of all
That I could claim as mine
One hundred percent of all I am
I give to the Divine

How can I give You everything?
All that I've ever known
To truly give You all of me
I must give up control

Bad things could happen now to me
And I'll have no defenses
I'll have to relax and let it be
And trust in You to mend it

But really if I give all to You
Putting myself at Your mercy
This is when I'm safest, sure
And Your glory I will see

For when in trials and circumstance
I'm safe inside Your hand
Nothing can really come against
And alter Your perfect plan

And so, in losing I will win
By giving up my life
For to receive I must give
I trust You; I've decided.

Constant Presence

Wherever I go, I find You
You are surrounding me
Within myself I see Truth,
You are the One who frees

I don't have to labor to enter Your Presence
For it is here I always dwell
You have not allowed any to be lost
Who are Yours to know full well

Relationship brings such beauty
Such glory in You I express
For just by letting You be
I become Your original best

I am a queen regnant eternal
But only in relation to You
You are the King of Creation
You are the Spirit of Truth

Wherever we go, we're together
Creation must us recognize
Submitting to the Word of Truth
That has already conquered all lies

There is no need for a battle
There is only need to remember
We had victory from our inception
And nothing can ever us hinder.

Entering Entirety

When the enemy says that I am lacking
I do not have to cower
For I remember what is true:
I've universal power

So, if I lack, I can receive
Yahweh's total entirety
If only I have eyes to see
What Yahweh's placed inside of me

So, I press on and I press in
Thus, entering entirety
A victory I know I'll win
For Holy Spirit's inside of me

Christ, my wisdom, all my power
I know my full entirety
For Yahweh's given all to me
I shall not settle for less than this!

There is always so much more
There's no shame to admit it
All I must do is throw open the door
What You have for me, I'll get it

You've given me tenacity
The strength to carry on
Nothing can stop the Spirit in me
I will keep on and keep on

This fiery passion's not from me
I didn't create this power
But what You give, I fully receive
I'll never again have to cower

I shall arise and I shall move on
In fullness, I will prosper
I have the faith to please my Father
I will not stop moving forward

Like a rocket, I shall ascend
Fueled by the vision
Protected by Christ's lordship
I will not stop until it is finished

I am not one who ever settles
I know what's Yahweh's best
Once the fire has tested my mettle
I will be fully blessed

Once in power I've pressed in
I will remember fullness
The entirety of Yahweh's Promise
Is mine now in this moment

Then You remind me that I'm free
Your simplicity takes over
Forgetting all that Babylon's taught me
I rest now in my Father

In perfect peace, You whisper love
In perfect truth, I breathe
In perfect grace, I am enough
To perfect love receive.

Remember

Right Now

Right now, I am in Yahweh's rest
Right now, I have all power
Right now, I'm all I need to be
Right now, I'm inspired

Right now, I've truth, peace, and grace
Right now, I'm a trueborn son
Right now, I operate in faith
Right now, I know everything's done

Right now, I'm Yahweh's anointed one
Right now, I am a Christ
Right now, I value what Yahweh loves
Right now, I am alive

Right now, I represent the Kingdom in the Earth
Right now, I show the love of the Father
Right now, I give what I've received
Right now, I choose to prosper

Right now, I'm thankful for all that is
Right now, I worship Yahweh
Right now, I have my Father's heart
Right now, I live in Today

Right now, I hear the Father's voice
Right now, I am complete
Right here and now I make a choice
Right here I am going to see

Right now, I'm accepted and approved
All for what Yahshua did
Right now, I know that I can't lose
What my elder Brother did win.

The Power of Relationship

Eternal omnipotent power
The resident power of Christ
Nothing can stop the Kingdom
In one Christ Identifies

Only in relationship to Him
Who in us the Promise has made
Can we do anything in the Earth
As we relate to Him by Faith

The power of Christ is within me
Even as I relate to Him
Who has all the power to give me
And I will receive what He gives

I honor the Christ that's within me
Fully submitted in grace
The victory is set before me
I am willing to go all the way

Relationship gives revelation
The vision of fullness to show
I must give up my former ways
If I am the fullness to know

I am to inherit the Kingdom
I am to remember the Way
To abide in established freedom
And walk in the Earth every day

I know what I know without doubting
What to me Holy Spirit does show
The holy, omnipotent power of Christ
That all of creation will know.

To Return a Promise

Whatever it takes, I will choose You
Whatever You ask I shall give
I know now that I cannot lose You
And though I may die, I shall live

My heart beats only for Your pleasure
I shall care for this vessel of Earth
For now, I can value the Treasures
That You placed in me before birth

Together we walk in creation
As one, united, hand in hand
Redeeming each tribe, tongue, and nation
Uniting the beasts, herbs, and land

I will go back to the Beginning
The place where it also shall end
For I will have faith in Your Promise
And I will be as You command.

R e m e m b e r

To Change the World

How can I change this world I'm in?
With all of its sorrows and pains
How can I matter or a difference make?
When all around me chaos reigns?

Trust in the Spirit, the fire within
The seed of redemption will grow
Planted inside the pure heart of man
So all of creation can know

First, we receive it and then we release it
So then others, too, can receive
The world will then change as we rearrange
All that is just because we believe

Faith changes all one step at a time
One decision, a choice to be made
As step-by-step we lay down our lives
And walk as Christ every day

Trusting the Spirit that dwells inside
He guides us each step of the way
Know that He is only ever good
And if we follow Him all is okay

To change the world is only to trust
In the Father who shows us His heart
To believe that He is in control of all things
That He's had a plan from the start

Then take my place in the original plan
Where I was made to be all along
To be who I'm called, who I really am
To sing to the world Yahweh's song

Oh, the glory that comes when things fit into place
When we submit to Yahweh's design
When each thread in the tapestry Yahweh creates
Has the faith to with Yahweh align

The world has to change, but to Yahweh's plan
For without the Word nothing good is
But when the Word comes, with Spirit and faith
The original Promise shall live.

R e m e m b e r

To Illuminate the Darkness

Yahweh is light, the glory we see
Expressing Himself in creation
As we see Him, we can come to be
His glorious manifestation

He calls us to shine and to illuminate
He said darkness can't overcome
When we allow Him in us to create
His own glorious image: a son

Creation is grand, with Creator we make
We partner with glory Himself
Casting out darkness by being the light
So, Creator in creation dwells

Oh, glorious light! Oh, great partnership!
Oh, trueness of glory's design!
Oh, to be part of all that there is
To find the place that's always been mine

To return to the Garden, to our Promised Land
To fear no giant or snake
To know that it's finished, at last I am home
To relate with the One who creates

Oh glory, oh victory, significance won
To exist as a part of the whole
All darkness is conquered, remembrance mine
The Creator never lost control

Oh worship, oh praise, oh illumination
Oh existence, oh coming to be
Oh, light in the darkness, oh great jubilation
Oh, thank You for returning to me!

Firestorm (To Fuel the Fire)

It may look like just an ember
But only if you don't look deep
If you have faith to remember
He will give you eyes to see

The fire deep inside you
The passion to ignite
When Holy Spirit resides in you
He will give your vision flight

The flames within your spirit
Shall burst forth into glory
As they draw upon the oxygen
And become a firestorm

Not waiting on the wind to blow
Creating its own tempest
The firestorm will strike a blow
To all that stands against it

Swirling and unstoppable
The passion deep inside
When Holy Spirit's given to full
Manifestation of Christ

Pressing forward, ever upward
We will advance the Kingdom
No one will think we're just an ember
When we manifest His freedom

There will be no denying
The power that will awe
When we express Yahweh fully
And allow Him to be God

Growing in glory and brightness
Like the firestorm we are
We will not stop until we see
All Yahweh's got in store.

Remember

To Take a Risk to Grow

Submitting to Christ's Lordship
Letting Holy Spirit reign
Begins only in worship
As we, like Jacob, seek Your face

Oh Yahweh, I so value
What You say and who You are
And the fact that You should even care
To live inside my heart

All it takes now I surrender
All I have is fully Yours
For You gave me to remember
What everything is for

All it takes, I know it's worth it
And I willingly apply
To be the True Son of my Father,
Even now to die

Growing deeper, ever greater
Learning all that You reveal
Knowing who I am and all You plan
Is much more than what I feel

Seeing all Your revelation
How it all just comes together
Gives me the courage to step out
And be part of Your forever

Holy Spirit, thank You Father
For allowing me to see
That just as I value Your Word
You also do value me

Willingly You take the risk
To make me now a son
You have a vision You won't dismiss
For it and I are one

The vision of maturity
For Your Ecclesia and Bride
Is greater to You than anything
For this You gave Your life

For it is part of the revelation
For us to in You grow
So that we can take our places,
Part in the vision's whole

Thank You for a purpose
Thank You for a place
Thank You for revelation
Which I fully embrace.

From the Moment

From the moment you were born
I set out to find you
I laid out My plans for
Your life to remind you

I loved you from the start
From the moment in My mind
When I spoke you into being
And called you to be Mine

And then I sent you out
My world to rediscover
But you should never doubt
That I have always been your Lover

From the moment you said yes
I had a joy unending
That I now share with you
For all broken things are mending

Then you began to grow
Into who I always made you
As you did come to know
All that I called you to

And I said, "Take your place"
And glory did arise
When you stepped out in faith
And gave to Me your life

From that moment on you lived
And grew into new stature
I will call you again
My dreams to chase after

Growing then in life
One step on another
But always without strife
Knowing I'm your Father

In each moment, I am yours
In each moment, you are Mine
Each moment you employ
A facet of the divine

I have such joy in you
Each moment I will share
All I have I give to you
A love beyond compare.

Remember

Greater Glory

The glory of the Father shows
When the son will take his place
When we are who He has called
And we operate in grace

The glory of the Father grows
As the son presses on through
As even in the harder times
The son the Word does choose

The glory of the Father lives
It moves and it has being
The glory is always His
This glory is you and me

The glory of the Father is
Was and will always be
Circumstances cannot change
The glory that's within me

The glory of the Father reigns
Over all created beings
The sovereignty of Yahweh
Will always be seen

The glory of the Father gains
As each son stands in faith
Laying down His life to increase
His government's embrace.

Remember

Laying Down Your Life

I am filled to saturation.
Overwhelmed with the goodness and vision
And love of my Father
I live in such blessing and yet have such
Frustration because I sense something more
On the horizon
I need it.
I need a deeper level of intimacy
Yet I know Yahweh gives me all I need
This is what it means to trust
To not go after for myself
What Yahweh gives me when I trust Him.
It is time to know, to practice believing
That He is faithful to bring me all of Himself
And everything I sense on the horizon,
To quietly wait patiently and know
That even in the waiting I am loved
Even in the waiting, I can have peace
Even in the waiting, there is a quiet time
Of rest
And I can
Be still and know
And maybe there's value in waiting
Yahweh is not impatient
And only in the waiting times can I learn all I have to learn and
Be still and know that He is God and I am me
And we are together
And perhaps the waiting is okay
If we do it together
And an intimacy and trust can grow in this place
Much more and much better than in any other
And I can grow here, too

For the waiting is Your tool, too, isn't it Yahweh?
And You have never minded to wait.

Upon the Ocean (Song of the Faith Dancer)

The ocean is vast and deep
With waves surrounding me
But when I look I can see
That it's Your glory crashing over me

And I will dance upon the ocean
Where once I never thought I'd stand
And I will see that for which I believed
As I receive what You command

Looking down under the water
I can see only so far
Swirling sand and shipwrecked plans
The remnants of the faint of heart

Looking up above the water
The horizon lies in front of me
There's no end when I do not relent
And choose to take a step and breathe

So, I will dance upon the ocean
Where I never even thought to stand
And I will go as far as You will show
And I will hold Your vision in my hand

Because the boat is far behind me now
I cannot see the shore
There is only wat'ry death
Or choosing to move forward

You are as faithful on the ocean
As You were when I was on the beach
When You called me out, told me to cast off doubt
And take a step of faith to truly see

That I can dance upon the ocean
You've made me capable and strong
This is the next step toward Your very best
So, I will dance and sing faith's song
Upon the ocean.

Dimensions

I give the oceans to explore
I call you out beyond the shore
All that you have, I give you more
You can't imagine what I've in store

Upon the ocean, you will dance
If you give your faith a chance
To arise beyond all circumstance
And in My presence, take a stand

Sometimes I call you out to swim
To dive so deep and enter in
To know My Love will always win
You will not drown; in Me you'll live

I give you oceans to explore
All that I've hidden, it is yours
It won't be kept from you anymore
You will find it and you'll soar

To a new dimension you will rise
For now, I've given you the skies
And spirit wings on which to fly
A holy purpose you make sight

I've hidden treasures here for you
I know that you will find them too
No matter what I call you to
You will be faithful to hear and do

Then you soar beyond the sky
Above the atmosphere you rise
Higher than the highest height
Greater perspective, brand new eyes

Exploring all of time and space
As My Holy Spirit, you embrace
All that I am is in this place
And in the mirror, you see My face

The greatest regions of My Heart
It is My joy now to impart
To one who'll finish what I start
Who longs for Me with their own heart

The greatest gift that I could give
Is Me, Myself, your place to live
Where all that will be, was, and is
Abides forever, Heaven's bliss.

Remember

Quiet Word

Yahweh, You are beautiful and worth it all and glorious
I am pressing in
But in the meantime, I will know Your love is still victorious
I just want more of it

Oh, Holy Spirit, speak you now, I am ready to listen
I do so want to hear
Whatever it is You have to tell and all that I am sensing
So, I will wait right here

I will trust in Your quiet Word as much as in the telling
You do not cease to speak
You are here in all I've heard, Your revelation dwelling
You live inside of me

The power is not altered in the volume of the speaking
It cannot ever change
It is inherent in the very nature of Your deity
The fruit that will remain

So, grow my faith and whisper now if whisper it You must
You gave me ears to hear
And if Your truth I must search out, well to the depths or bust!
You will make all things clear.

The Bride's Song

Infinite expanses beyond all time and space
Glorious access to all we enter now by faith
Faithful intercession by Yahshua for His Bride
Powerful expression when she will lay down her life

Greater is the glory as the Kingdom will increase
Not just over time and space, but first it grows in me
Oh manifestation, oh conqueror of doubt
Oh the faith to substance make and magnify His sound

Intimacy, cry of my heart, oh deepest soul desire
All that's outward comes from this, relating to the fire
There is only this embrace in creation we will see
That which Yahweh purposed and placed and called out into being

All that is and ever was to Holiness submitting
Receiving truth and endless love, from all this benefitting
Flowing in the Spirit's power, growing into freedom
Becoming what was in His mind as He spoke each Word of creation.

Writing

Scrolling through the Internet, looking at the world
The pictures
The ugly, but mostly the good
And suddenly, I felt like writing
I felt like I was so blessed and honored to be chosen by my God
To be able to worship Him in writing
To be able to relate to Him at all
And suddenly, I felt like writing
A song from the radio playing in my head
Telling of what Yahweh's done
How He's redeemed me, saved me,
Made me a Promise
How I am so blessed to be chosen by my God
For redemption and a purpose
And a relationship with Him
And suddenly, I felt like writing
Remembering where I have been
What Yahweh's called me out from
How I was so lost and broken
And I didn't even know who I was
That He loved me and He wants me
That He would tell me this at all
And suddenly, I felt like writing
Sitting in my comfy chair,
A dog right there next to me
Nothing to do but to be free
And live in the Father's love for me
And suddenly, I feel like writing
So, I write this poem
As worship to my God
And gratitude for all He is
That I can relate to Him at all

It's a miracle
It's worth writing about.

Discovery

It's amazing how we can see
The beauty of Your Majesty
In all creation's tapestry
In each and every thread

How marvelous that we can know
Your glory in a river's flow
And how every speck of dirt can show
All of Heaven's depth

In every bird we see in flight
In how the darkness flees the light
The very fact that we have sight
Demonstrates freedom won

All You called and made to be
Contains a portion of Your being
Truth encased in Earthly seed
For all in You is One

As we walk out in this land
We learn to see in circumstance
The Power of Your righteous hand
Your vision You will teach

The beauty of Your ornaments
A love that never will relent
A redemption lies cannot prevent
The joy of discovery

The glory when we take our place
In the fullness of Heaven's embrace
And operate in power's grace
And all things work together

For when each part will demonstrate
The glory for which it was made
Then all creation can operate
As it was always meant to.

Remember

Declarations

Declarations resonate
In every molecule of time and space
When you speak the Word of Yahweh aloud
All of creation will cry out

Reminding you of what you said
That the Word of Yahweh is not dead
Your calls become creation's essence
For the glory of Yahweh is hidden within

We've all heard that creation cries
With groans that we can't recognize
Until the sons will take their place
And hear what creation has to say

Creation is reminding you
Being a witness to the Truth
That what Yahweh spoke before time
Is a living Word and still alive

When you are tempted to forget
Creation will have none of it
So declare the Word that you now know
So creation has something to echo

The sons will hear creation's cries
Remove the veil, shake off the lies
For all that Yahweh's hidden there
Cannot be moved; become aware

When you call forth Yahweh's deep Truth
It will resonate back to you
It will start a fire from a spark
And all will see the Father's heart

The hidden glory shall be revealed
For what Yahweh spoke can't be repealed
It echoes in every tribe and nation
It is spoken by all of creation

Resonating throughout space and time
The original Word of the Divine
Unhidden, pure, and undefiled
Heard by those with the faith of a child

We hear His Word and echo, too
Passing on His hidden Truth
So that the Word goes deep into
All that He made; it's through and through.

Access and Awareness

I have access and awareness to all the universe in Christ
I have been given vision, I can see with Yahweh's eyes
In the blades of grass, in the specks of dirt, in the birds that fly in the
skies
I have access and awareness to all the universe in Christ

I have access and awareness to all the resources in universe in Christ
For Yahweh is my Father; He says I did not leave you here to die
I said I would come back for you, I did lay down My Life
I gave you access and awareness to all the power of the universe in Christ

You are purposed and you're promised, you have everything you need,
All the resources in Heaven I have placed now at your feet
And as you continue on your path, it shall become clear and seen
Stand in faith, walk on, keep going, and discover mysteries in Me

You have access and awareness to all My resources in Christ
I have laid them out before you in the pathway of your life
Then I gave to you My Spirit to live with you inside
To teach you how to use the power that I gave you in My Christ

He has taught you how to see it, He has given you My eyes
And awareness leads to access which leads to resources for life
Every resource is an assignment, which gives you even more light
To see more resources that were hidden but by faith shall be made
sight

You have access and awareness to everything that's Me
For I have not left you as orphans, I have given you eyes to see
I am the Creator of the Universe and I came back to set you free
And give you access and awareness to everything that's Me

Praise Yahweh for the awareness that He's given me tonight
Awareness of the access that is Yahshua's life
Now there's an open door of blessing that for me operates inside
And I have access and awareness to all the universal resources in Christ.

Remember

Speak

Two days ago, I spoke a Word,
Declared the Truth of Yahweh
Then last night, the enemy tried
To make me forget what I said

This morning I did arise
and speak the Word again
For I want all to see and remember with me
The Truth that dwells within

And as I chose Truth, something in me arose
The faith of Yahweh prevailed
I began to listen and to hear
Yahweh speak again

He spoke through creation, He told me the Truth
He reminded me of the Promise
In all circumstances, in stories, in you
He said, "Nothing is ever lost"

So, I will remember what I did declare
Even if the enemy tries to trick me
I won't believe him, he lies and he fails
Instead I listen to Yahweh when He speaks.

Remember

Heart of a Writer

I want to write!
I want to process the things that have happened,
I want to discover Yahweh in the midst of it all
I want to worship Him for He is still good and He is still God.

I want to write!
I want to lay out my thoughts in an orderly fashion
So that I can make sense of them all
I want to listen to Yahweh and discover His revelation
For He is still good and He is still God.

I want to write!
I want to inscribe the Truth in immutable form
I want to read it again later when I'm tempted to forget
I want to leave behind a legacy for future generations
To read and discover Him, too.

I want to write!
I want to live!
I want to be worship and praise to my God!
I want to show all that He is who He is
And that in Him nothing can ever be lost.

I want to write!
And oh! My God is so wonderful because
He calls me to do the very thing that is in my heart to do
But of course He does,
For He placed it there Himself.

I want to write!
So, I write.
I worship Yahweh as I write
And take my place.
I live in Him.
I praise Him.
I thank Him.
Thank You that I can write!

Remember

Wings

To take a leap on faith-blown wind
Is to use your wings to fly
You were always made for this
For this you are alive

What good are wings upon the land
Why have them if not to soar
You've been given this command
Your talents not to store

So be not afraid to flap your wings
For flight is guaranteed
It only seems a scary thing
Before you take the leap

But oh! To rise upon the winds
Over all creation to soar
You know that you've found your purpose
All that you were created for

To find your place in the Promised skies
Is worth a leap of faith
So, do not give in to the lies
Rise up and live in grace.

Let There Be

A Word… Bam! Existence
When You said, "Let there be"
Creation sprung up from Your mind
A testament to Your beauty

The fire of Your passion
Then took on different forms
Spreading out through time and space
A universe was born

In all that was created
The fire's light still burns
Giving life to all that is
And around it all things turn

Each flame seeks out another
For all things seek their own
But when seeking You it finds
It has a lasting home

For all that was created
Shares a facet of the One
Who spoke and made the finished work
And started what was done

And as flames join together
They become a firestorm
Raging on to sanctify
All that ever was

You're returning all creation
To its original form
Redeeming all tribes and nations
So though different, they are one

Completing then the picture
That was born inside Your mind
When first You spoke the Word aloud
And said, "Let there be light!"

In the Interim

Trust
To know that the Truth that's hidden
Shall be revealed
As by faith we remove the illusion
That tries to cover what,
By its very nature,
Cannot help but shine through

Oh, magnificent Creator!
That You would hide a piece of Yourself in creation
To come forth in just the right time
And finish creation
Redeem creation
Secure creation
So that it could not be lost
No matter what happened in the interim

Holy Spirit
Working on the inside
To show the Truth of creation
To itself
So that it could come into agreement with the Truth that it's seen
And become what it's always been
What it was in the Beginning when You said
"Let it be."

Remember

Justice

How is it justice for You to lose creation
And how by rights can we not be of You
How is it righteous for every tribe and nation
To listen to the enemy and lose

But You who right all wrongness
And from darkness bring the light
Have come to recover all things lost
And on a cross You gave Your life

You brought justice out of madness
You received victory from loss
When in chaos all did die
You paid in full the cost

Then somehow grace is truly justice
In You all loss is truly gain
And underneath what seems like rot
Is a fruit that will remain

Only You, Yahweh, can bring glory
From what the enemy did choose
And only in Your Holy Christ
Can we win even though we lose

Thank You, Yahweh, HalleluYah!
For the certainty of Your Truth
For foundations that cannot be lost
For returning us to You!

Remember

Petty Satisfactions

I will not be satisfied
With less than all of Yahweh's Christ
With less than the fullness of life
Of all that Yahweh's called me

I will not settle for less
Than all that Yahweh has promised
Than Yahweh's original best
This is what I will be

So, I will stand and take my place
Live the life that Christ dictates
His Truth all else obliterates
So, in Him I'll take action

My life will not be negated
I will not by less be elated
For I never was created
For such petty satisfactions.

Remember

Growing and Learning

The process of discovery
Of learning of Your love
Of becoming who You made me
Of knowing that's enough

Looking beyond the surface
To find the Truth inside
Knowing we have all the victory
And death cannot trump life

That whatever comes against it,
Your Truth shall ever be
And when illusion is destroyed
We see Reality

Sometimes destruction is redemption
And to live one has to die
But we have hope for resurrection
And put an end to all the lies

Then all can see the glory
That once was hid within
It becomes obvious and manifests
So we see only what truly is.

Thus

Thus the plan was so envisaged
Thus created and laid out
Thus spoken into existence
Thus the Truth came out

Thus the glory of the Father
Thus the beauty deep inside
Thus was lavished on another
Thus at once Life came alive

Thus it was unchanged, immutable
Thus unable to be touched
Thus it still is operational
Thus, ever victorious

Thus it was at the Beginning
Thus ever it shall be
Thus the Truth is never ending
Thus it is eternally!

Thus illusion all that's opposite
Thus these lies can never be
Thus the Truth comes out and manifests
Thus, creation is set free

Thus the plan that was envisioned
Is still thus and thusly is
Thus, Reality's existence
Is not in question; thus, we live!

Contrary

In opposition to the contrary actions
Of the government and society of this world,
Which has chosen to run counter
To the Truth established before time
I stand

In regards to the contrary choices made
By the mind that has believed the lies
And which try to oppose the Truth
That, being established, cannot be disestablished,
I cry foul

In repentance of all the choices I have made
When I was unaware of Truth myself,
Though Truth was unaltered within me
Having been established before time
I change

In gratitude for the revelation of that Truth
And the ability to see and receive it in myself
Beyond illusory lies that tried to tell me that
Something had changed the immutable Truth that was
Established before time
I am.

Remember

Groan

The trials and pains that come up in this life
Clamor and yell for attention
Then we start to groan, agitate, and moan
And attempt to avoid with prevention

But Reality's strong when we look deep inside
Distractions can't move it; it's hidden
But we who are sons have Spiritual Life
A free gift that to us was given

Yahweh's Truth is strong if we with it agree
Then we become fruit that remains
If we give up illusion and focus on Truth
We will have infinite gains

So we join with the Truth and we will become
Who Yahweh always made us to be
We will be glory as our Father's true Word
So, sow to the Spirit and see!

Remember

I Will Press On To See

Old ideas struggle and try to arise
Old mindsets try to grow
Old worries and fears try to distract me
Old ways ask me in them to flow

But I have been shown there's a better way now
And I have been freed of these lies
There is a Truth that is more real than these
Old ways that try to arise

So I will rise higher and take a stand in my place
Where the Truth gives perspective new life
I will prophesy and declare this to be
A Truth that will be brought to light

I will keep going 'til fullness is won
Until His Truth's manifesting in me
Then the whole world will notice the Truth that there is
Because I will press on to see.

To Receive Beforehand

I see a world where Yahweh's Truth reigns
Where there is no sickness or doubt
Where nobody thinks that they're less than they are
A world where not one is left out

Here all the people are secure in the Truth
In the love of the Father for them
Then in security they love others too
And give all the first and the best

We can appreciate Yahweh's great grace
In others as well as ourselves
We value all that Yahweh did create
For in all of creation He dwells

He hid His beauty in all things to find
A discovery awaiting it's time
And once we find it we give it new life
As in Him we learn how to shine

For I have now seen it and now I receive it
I have the faith to believe
I join with others who've seen it as well
And we live in this world that we've seen

A world without suffering, without right and wrong
Where lies never will be believed
Where all is how Yahweh wanted it all along
And the Father's gift of Life is received

And we are so grateful for this Life that He gave
But He gave it out more than once
When He first spoke creation, He gave life being
And again when He died on the cross

But this world that I see and so fully receive
Is worth anything it might cost
It's a world that was Promised when we came to be
For Yahweh's Truth cannot be lost!

Vision's Hope

The Truth that remains, though lies tried to hide
I can see it, therefore I am hope
I am hope that this Truth shall be revealed in time
And that Yahweh doesn't change what He spoke

The enemy can only hide the Truth with a lie
He does not have the power to change it
He can only make us worry and fret
But the Truth is still as Yahweh made it

So, I will believe in the Truth that I see
And the lies will not cause me to be wonder
Because Yahweh's Truth will be seen in me
I will conquer the enemy and plunder

Just by having hope, being faithful in this Truth
I conquer the lies and distractions
The enemy was always fated to lose
As soon as Yahweh's sons give faith action

So natter on, enemy, I will not hear you
I will not believe any lies that you speak
I will stand firmly on Yahweh's sure Truth
And your lies will fall at your own feet!

Remember

The Voice

You speak through the sunshine glistening through trees
And when the leaves rustle, You speak through the breeze
You speak through the waters that through rivers flow
And when we will trust You, You speak in all we know

You speak through our choices, You speak through our lives
You speak in all voices that in praise arise
You speak in vision and You speak Your Truth
But whatever You speak through, Your Word is You

We hear Your prompting and we know Your Word
Then we too will shout forth the Word that we've heard
All that You created becomes then Your voice
You're always speaking, no matter the noise

You speak through our children, the next generation
You speak through every tribe, tongue, and nation
We hear You speaking, we count it all joy
And as we receive You, we become Your Glory.

Into the Depths

Your river of life in vastness before me
Such profundity calling me in
The depths of Your wisdom in essence undoes me
And I become One with what is

I flow in Your River as Your River flows through me
My Being again One with You
All that I am in the I AM baptized
Thus unity is through and through

Nothing that's in me remains above water
I don't even come up to breathe
For what breath have I lest You breathe in my nostrils
In You I have all that I need

Truth drowns experience, lies, circumstances
All that remains is Your Word
Who I am, pure in You, triumphs and lives
As from Your great depths I emerge

Then I take You on, now a branch of Your River
Flowing out into all that You made
From my belly flows life, peace, joy, righteousness
Again, You reach all You create

Baptizing new souls into Your Holy Spirit
Showing all what it means to be free
Trusting that we can't drown if we choose to die
Knowing in You we will always be.

Remember

Spectacles

The darkness that pervades the night,
Covering the world
Is broken by a simple light:
Your glory now unfurled

Glory is to see You more
Revealing You in worship
That under all that's dark and dour
Lies an unaltered foundation

Then tapping into the light that is
We can become Your glory
Shining brightly, we can't be missed
As we tell the world Your story

Babylon, it looks to die
But it was dying always
Now Your Kingdom can arise
As Your Bride ascends in faith

We are the alternative
Because we see the Truth
Looking through faith's spectacles
Your glory in us shines through

Then we become the spectacles
That through us others see
For we are pure receptacles
For Yahweh's Truth to be

When all around us kingdoms fall
And nations seem to tumble
We of faith will still stand tall
And shine in the midst of rubble

So come and be a spectacle
Let all eyes fall on you
For when of the Spirit you are full
You give Promise the proof

Evidence of what's not seen
We give substance to hope
When we become what Yahweh dreamed
Then all the world can know.

Remember

Sabbath Sight

Worshipping the Father, resting sure in Him
Knowing that we can have hope if we see His vision
Abiding in His Presence as we value who He is
Nothing can come from the outside to alter what He says

There is such peace in knowing, tranquility and rest
That nothing ever really is but what Yahweh Promised
The voices from the outside are silenced and unheard
The only thing that I can hear is Yahweh's spoken Word

The beauty of the vision I see when I with Yahweh dwell
Gives me hope and joy to carry on as in Him my heart swells
No matter what the enemy tries to tell me with his lies
I know the Truth is all I see when I have Yahweh's eyes

Then I become what I have seen, I then the vision cast
So all can know and testify that only His Truth lasts
The Truth of Yahweh keeps me safe as I abide in Christ
So in His Presence I will stay and see with Sabbath Sight.

Eternal Satisfaction

The depth of longing from my soul
The desire inside to be made whole
To know my Father true in full
The joy of revelation

To become all I'm called to be
To look at the world and still have peace
To from all hindrance become free
To be a new creation

To in my purpose find my place
To operate in unlimited grace
To stand immovable in faith
To build a holy nation

To Kingdom Truth perpetuate
To be a portal, open gate
To leave a legacy so great
For future generations

To in My Father learn and grow
And from His Spirit, glorious flow
To have the Truth and knowing, know
A holy impartation

Satisfied with the Father's love
Who I am in Him, enough
All that is, to Him I trust
For new regeneration

With my Father now relating
Never in Him hesitating
Yahweh's plan, my hunger sating
This is my jubilation.

Remember

"Let There Be Light"

The Promise is poised, waiting
The plan is laid out, extended in all directions
There is silence.
Darkness hovers over the face of the deep.
All that Yahweh desires in place, waiting
Ready
Every nuance in place; every Promise made.
We agitate in the Spirit, unseen
Excited
For we know that time and space is coming
Our Father will speak.
We joy, exult
We are sure
We are sure of Yahweh's Promise—
who we are, what we are for, that we have all
the tools we need—and we are complete.
We are jubilant! Even though
We know what's coming
And all that we have to go through
But we have heard the Promise
And in agreement, we became the Promise
So we are finished and sure
And our Father is poised to speak
And reveal all that already is:
All that He Promised
So we listen, ready to go, as He says,
"Let there be light!"

Remember

What I Knew

Did I know all that my life was going to be
Was I aware of everything that You promised me
Did I see the vast expanse of time and space
Did I know the beauty of all that You chose to create

Did my heart break with Yours at the fall
And in Your redemption, did I with You exult
They say the joy of the LORD is my strength
Did I then share with You in everything

Did I know all of the pain that I would feel
Did I desire Your creation with Your passionate zeal
Was I excited just to be a part
Of the world that You created from Your very heart

Did I see the entire tapestry in Your eyes
Before the fall and all the enemy's horrible lies
Did I know the Beginning and the End
Is that why I agreed when me You thought to send

Did I know that it would be worth the fight
Did I know there would be darkness when I only knew the Light
Was I aware of all that it was going to cost
Did I watch and weep with You as You died on the cross

Oh to remember what I knew before time
Oh to see again with the eyes of the Divine
Oh to recall the Promise that You made
When You set me down and chose to create

When You showed me Your creation in such array
When You said that it was good at the end of each day
When You were so excited to finally see
What You purposed in Your heart and then said, "Let there be"

When You shared with me Your vision for my life
When You gave me all the tools to conquer the lies
When You chose to make me in Your heart
When You Promised that we'd never again be apart

Did I know then what I cannot understand
Did I see all of the nuances of Your master plan
Did I weep with the burdens of the lost
Did I sing HalleluYah when You died on the cross

Did I know then that it would be worth it all
Well, I remember the Promise that You made after all
You said that You would always love me
And that I would be made perfect when I chose to believe

I would come back to the place where I did know
I would become a fountain of Your righteous Love
All would be exactly as You planned
And I would be better for it in the end

Yes, I knew all that my life was going to be
I had certainty of everything You Promised to me
I saw and loved the world that You created
And to be able to have a part made me elated

I had the LORD's own joy for You did share it
You told me everything, I was made fully aware and
I will not be moved by circumstances
Because this gift of remembering, I'll never take for granted

And I will know again what I then knew
And I will see again Your righteous Truth
And I will share Your life with all creation
So we can conquer the lies as a holy convocation.

Remember

Spirit-Man

There is a part of me that remembers
Inside of me right now
That heard the Promise complete, entire
And saw it all laid out

Who knew from the Beginning
Even to the End
And saw what I have not yet seen
Even all of completion

She saw all the steps of the process
Everything that is still yet to be
She has the faith to carry on
And see what I've not yet seen

This part of me that remembers
What I knew long before time
Is the part to whom I give control,
The leader of my life

My spirit, One with Yahweh
For He allowed me so to be
When He came and laid upon the cross
And gave His Life for me

Remembering the Promise
The fullness of the Word
And everything that Yahweh said
When first He made the world

Then I walk out my purpose
Taking each step of faith
Knowing Yahweh's Word is True
And He's provided grace

There's no such thing as failure
When my spirit-man's in charge
For she values Yahweh above all
Enough to carry on

To see the Truth of Yahweh
Make it manifest by faith
So what I saw long before time
Will again be seen today.

Remember

Confirmed Promise

When Yahweh spoke the Promise
Of my life before all time
He said He would give His all
To keep it

But I must be the Promise
For it to come true in my life
For every Promise requires
Full agreement

So with the fullness of His Promise
I will choose now to agree
So I can see the Promise
Of my Father

For I know now that a Promise
Is really a two-way street
And I will choose to give
The Promise honor.

Yahshua

The High Priest of our confession
The Firstborn of many brethren
The Word spoken before time
The express image of the divine

Yahweh's glory in the Earth
In the Beginning, Him the Word
Son of God, Son of Man
He is still the Great I AM

Holy Mediator, King and Priest
Without Him, nothing could be
In Him, all things are One
Oh, only begotten Son

Doing only what the Father did
Authoring what He finished
For joy He endured the cross
So Yahweh's Promise would not be lost

Elder Brother, Firstborn Son
In Him is all our redemption
Give Him honor, for He is life
All hail Yahshua the Christ!

Remember

Hopes and Dreams

What if our true hopes and dreams
Are flashes of memory
Desires for the very things Yahweh would give us,
Promised us
All along?

Power

The enemy did speak today
Again inside my mind
Telling me to be afraid
To give up and not try

Again I had a choice to make
To stand or run away
To listen and believe the snake
Or believe instead Yahweh

So I will stand and thereby win
I will not faint or falter
In Yahweh's Truth I will live
For His Word cannot be altered

But I will be the activated
Power of Yahweh
I can never be defeated
If I take my place

For I have vision and the faith
To manifest perfection
And walking in the Earth today
I demonstrate resurrection

The Holy power of my God
My Lord and my Creator
Ensures the victory is won
And conquers all debaters

So when the loser tries to shout
And tell me that I can't win
I will simply cast him out
By refusing to listen.

Endless Well

There's an endless well of resources
Available to me
And a vessel to access
The fullness of the deep

Whenever I must make a draw
I know everything's available
I have all that I'll ever need
So of all things I am capable

I'm not a leaking vessel
For the resources to fall
So when I go to look for them
I know I'll have them all

Everything once purposed
And planned out for my life
Is already here for me
Just waiting deep inside

The Word, my Father's resources
Abiding in my heart
All I need my life to live
He did already impart

So I will use the resources
That they should not be wasted
And show the world that Yahweh is
Greater than what they've tasted

Taste and see that the LORD is good
Draw upon the Promise
This well shall never run dry
For Yahweh's a good Father.

Sovereign

Reign down upon me now
Stream Your Truth into my life
You have all sovereignty and power
Here and now I recognize

Ultimate trust in Your provision
Regardless of circumstance
We will not be altered or change
No matter what comes, we will stand

We do it together, always in You
Today You remove all my fear
I don't have to worry that I'm not enough
For I know that You are always here

Looking forward in unity
To all that we'll live out together
Knowing that as You build day on day
Each moment with You shall be better

I have all power to conquer the lies
But only 'cause You are within me
My DNA is that of Christ
So all of creation's submitting

In my metron I am sovereign
Only because I am one with You
So I submit to Your Lordship
And worship in Spirit and Truth!

Remember

Omnipotential

Inside
An ember glowing
Warm and bright
Waiting for the spark of faith
That will finally ignite

World-changing
Altering the fabric
Of time and space
Waiting for the sons of Yahweh
To finally embrace

Omnipotence
Active and working
In the Promised Land
Expertly wielded by the worshippers
Of the Great I AM

Omnipotential
Hidden in all visions
Of the Father's eyes
Creation growing, creation groaning
Waiting for the sons of Yahweh to arise.

Remember
____

DNA

All that we are encoded in genes
Spoken to life before time
In every one of the protein links
Is the pattern of the Divine

A language known only by Yahweh
Building blocks of creation
Slowly becoming His glory
As He reveals all to His sons

In each individual life form
Is an individual world
And everything in existence
Is an individual Word

As we learn to read Heaven's pattern
Discover the Truth that's inside
We will become Yahweh's Promise
And reflect Christ's phenotype

Then what's within shall be visible
Reality finally shown
Christ's DNA manifest in full
His Truth in totality known.

Body

Oh expression of who He is
The marvelous, glorious Christ
Throughout the body that is His
To which He gave His life

Each and every one of us
Is essential to His glory
So all His vision manifests
And the fullness of His story

I cannot deny who I am
For to do so robs the body
Of the fullness of the Father's plan
And the facet of Him that is in me

And I cannot deny the facet
Of the Christ inside of you
For so valuable is your expression
If I want to see all Truth

We are made complete together
The body of the Christ
And when we recognize each other
His hope is realized

Glory, glory, Yahweh's glory
As He makes the whole world One
For out of Oneness He made many
When He gave His only Son

To make many sons of Yahweh's Glory
To redeem what was stolen
So that nothing ever could be lost,
Taken from Him, or broken.

Remember

Warrior Queen

I am a warrior queen
Ruling and reigning where Yahweh placed me
And I know
Who I am and my part in the plan
Because I am a warrior queen

I am a victorious queen
All my dominion shall listen to me
And I know
That I've won for I am Yahweh's son
Because I am a victorious queen

I am Yahweh's Queen
In Him is my purpose and in Him is my being
And I know
What I say for it comes from Yahweh
For I am Yahweh's Queen

I am a glorious queen
Shining so brightly so all can see
And I know
My own light for it's Yahweh inside
Because I am a glorious queen

I am a noble queen
Walking with dignity and purity
And I know
Yahweh's Word for His voice I have heard
And I am a noble queen.

I Know

Remembering the Truth that was wrought before time
Having the mind of the divine
Knowing Reality's still alive
I have the faith in Yahweh to shine

And I know what I know can't be taken away
For all that I know is the Truth of Yahweh
And I know that I'll grow in this Truth every day
For I will receive the Spirit of grace

I remember what Yahweh spoke into being
When He first decided to create me
I will see the fullness of all He meant to be
For I will have faith to demonstrate peace

And I know what I know can't be taken away
And I know that I'll grow in Reality's faith
And I know that I'll show Yahweh's fullness today
For I have the faith of my Father Yahweh

And I will not forget the Truth I know
I'll remember His Word, and in Him I will show
All Reality's proof and all I need to know
For all that I have in me is Glory's Hope

And I know what I know won't be taken away
For no power on Earth could do such a thing
For my God and my King will stand with me always
And I will abide in unyielding faith.

Throne

There is a throne reserved for me
In my own place and time
It waits for me to reign as queen
Over the land that's mine

Once one did try to steal my throne
But I would not forget
That this place in the Kingdom is my own
And I would not let it be his

So I will sit upon my throne
And take my rightful place
But I don't have to reign alone
For I rule with Yahweh

It is His Kingdom and His power
But He has given me
The right to rule in this hour
To be His regnant Queen

Nothing on Earth can stop me now
And naught can overtake
The one that Yahweh has endowed
With the right to rule and reign.

Introspection

Today I want to look within
Find the power there
To know the Promise from the origin
The light beyond compare

And I, oh, I discover
An unwavering flame
Blazing Truth and fed with courage
Based in Yahweh's Name

Unassailable, this Truth
All creation must recognize
And bow before the authority
That deep in me resides

And I can stand upon this Word
My God's anointed power
It's in me, shining unperturbed
So cower, enemy, cower!

Try not to come against me now
For you can never win
You can't stand against what I have found
With my introspection.

Shepherd

The sheep, such value and potential
Such promise that I want to see
Realized in full

Oh the lengths to which I'll go
To reclaim that which was Mine
They stole

The desires of My heart well-known
Oh, sheep of My glory
You're not alone

Oh that the shepherd would die for His sheep
And that for a peasant is traded the life of a king
A lion for a lamb would be sacrificed
The greatest love of all is to lay down your life

It's not really a very difficult thing to do
When in peasants, lambs, sheep,
I can see the value

I see it for I created this value inside
In everything that I did make
I hid some of My Light

To Me it is worth it all; I knew the cost
When I first chose to make the world
Even then I saw the cross.

I Was There When It Was Written

Once upon the dawn of time
There was a written law
It was upon the occasion
Of all creation's fall

This written law did set in place
Such evil and such pain
All enmity, disease, and death
This law did then create

All of creation cried aloud
With all forms of expression
Oh come and rescue, save us now
From this horrible oppression!

Creation languished in dark despair
For many a thousand years
Until one day a Savior came
To eliminate all fears

He told us of a deeper law
Written long before time
A Promise that He did fulfill
This new law nullified!

There is a power that supersedes
There is a deeper Truth
The law written at the fall must bow
To the Promise that's in you

Remember now the Promise
That was written before all
It was unable to be changed
Or altered by the fall

The Promised Law is still in place
Operating still in full
All we must do is tap into it
To be made completely whole

For we were there long before the fall
When Yahweh's Promise was made
We saw Him write and spell it out
When He chose to create

So reread the original law
Written long before creation
Remind the world that it's possible
To tap into its operation

For tapping into this law's power
Answers creation's cry
And brings salvation to the land
Making everything again right.

Advance

Advance, adventure awaits!
I move forward and the enemy tries to drag me back again
He activates triggers, people, old mindsets
To try to get me to doubt myself
To stop
To halt
To cease to advance

But something greater beckons
And I am no longer subject to the lies and oppression
I remember
I remember the Truth that was placed in me before time
The Promise that Yahweh made
That is myself
That is my life
And I know that the only way I shall attain
Is to advance and advance and
To keep going

So I advance
For it is worth it
Everything I have to lose and all the pain that comes with loss
But there is so much joy set before me
And joy set within me now
A little flame of joy in my heart
Keeping me warm as I advance
Giving me strength as I advance
Urging me to keep going, to advance
So that I can see the fullness
Of all that little flame can be
Oh, the potential
This flame can light the nations

Can warm the hearts of all creation
This flame can change the world

So shouldn't I advance?
Is it not worth it to change the world,
To make it better?
We can be better.

This flame is worth it
The Reality of Yahweh
The Promise inside of me
The joy set within me
It is worth it! I must guard it!
I must protect this Truth
And it protects me, too
As I value it
I value Him
Above everything else in all of creation
For I know that I know that I know
That I know
That this flame is both the reason and
The method
To advance.

And I cannot wait to see
What this flame will be
When operating fully
In the glory of my King
For whom I advance.

Remember

A Father's Pride

When I see you carrying out the plans that I made for you before time,
Walking in the Promise, in the Truth of Your life
I consider all the glory and remember the joy
That was set before me when the cross I endured

When I see you operating in the righteous Way
On the path I came before you to set
I remember the very reason that I chose to make
You and send you to the Earth from Heaven

And I watch and I see the choices you've made
And I know that you've counted the cost
There have been many trials and, yes, even pain
And I'm glad that you wanted there to be an Us

I know that I'm worth it, but you know it too
There is nothing the enemy can then undo
So I will stand here beaming, yes stand by your side
Filled with the strength of a Father's Pride

I'm so happy to have you here with Me
And to know that you're so very dear
That you listen and obey whenever I speak
Allows Me to complete what you hear

So I stand right beside you, giving you strength
To operate in all of My Truth
Just know that I'm with you and you give Me joy
And I'm so very proud of you.

Remember

From the Mouth

From the mouth of Yahweh creation comes
Existence is framed by the Word
All that is and ever was
Reality has to be heard

For Yahweh has spoken since long before time
Calling His plan all together
But all that's created must hear and obey
If we are to see Truth forever

To the ears of all who are willing to hear
And choose to become Yahweh's pleasure
Electing with action to resonate with
His own heart's deep desired treasure

I am one who will hear spoken Truth
And become who I already am
One who will know Yahweh's profound depths
And carry out Heaven's plan.

Remember

The Joy of Being

The glory and joy of being true
To the reason that I was created
Of all of the excellence in what I do
Because I know that for which I was made

Flowing in Yahweh, my facet of Christ
Enjoying the Reality in me
Seeing much more than just with my eyes
Knowing the Word that does set free

Worshipping the One who created the Promise
Then elected the Promise to keep
Even though I did not always honor
Yahweh's true Promise in me

For He saw the value before I ever saw
He knew when He chose to create
Every nuance and every facet
Of His plan and His holy mandate

And though I'd forgotten, He came to remind me
Of the reason for which I exist
He showed me His glory that is deep inside me
And that is of what I consist

Oh! Heaven's glory, the joy of creation
Being One with my Father again
And out of that Oneness, what pure elation
What a gift of life is given!

Oh to be me in the fullness that Yahweh imagined
When He saw me inside of His mind
It is so much deeper than what I had fathomed
Even more than I now realize

So I remember the Promise that is to me entrusted
For He trusted me with myself
He wanted to know if I would choose to trust Him
With my life and everything else

So I give Him my existence and all that I am
And I worship in Truth and in Spirit
And in taking my place I fulfill His plan
Cast the vision to all who will hear it

The joy of knowing the full redeemed Promise
And knowing that I am indeed me
Knowing the Truth and the love of my Father
And His manifest Reality.

The Risk

It is worth the risk to find myself
To discover the Promise within
To remember who I always was
And be that person again

It is worth the risk to make a mistake
For I know that I cannot fail
In Yahweh, I will always be okay
For only His Word can prevail

So I will take a risk for my Promise
As Yahweh took a risk on me
He did not have to give me trust
To make the Promise full and complete

Recklessly, I will abandon all that I once
Thought I could not live without
For only what I am willing to lose
Will be mine without any doubt

It is worth the risk for the Promise
For the Word in which Yahweh delights
I will give Him the honor
Of taking this risk now tonight

Faithfully I will await the results
Of the risks that I will take by faith
I know that they will be beautiful
And that Yahweh's Promise will remain.

Remember

Never

It looked bad, like I would die
Like danger lurked on every side
It looked like horror, fear, and lies
But I have never lost a fight

I never really left Your arms
I was always safe from harm
Your plan always laid out for me
I was never anything but free

The hurt was there, the pain was real
But Reality's more than what I feel
I never Really was alone
I was always with You, home

There was never a chance my Promise to lose
I never chose anything other than You
Circumstances swirling, the world wants its say
But I was never anything but Yours, oh Yahweh

Never a loser, never lost
You provided victory for me on the cross
Never uncovered, always protected
Never anything less than love perfected

Never to be lacking, never without
Never was there any real doubt
For nothing can stop Your Promise from being,
Never anything than less than You made me to be

Never more than I am, never else but with You
Never having to live a life without fruit
Always, eternally, infinitely True
Always together, always One, never two.

Remember

Order

The intrinsic union with the divine
Nature's breath of Holy Life
Giving purpose to Earthly forms
In this way unity was born

We walked the coolness of the Day
And Sabbath rest we did create
Heaven and Earth together as One
No separation 'tween Father and son

All only subject to Love's pure law
All manifestation only what Yahweh saw
When He envisioned creation inside His mind's eye
The Garden of Eden of Him testified

Looming, the Promise covering above
Unable to be broken, abiding in love
All Truth and provision fully to be seen
No need to toil to bring harvest from seed

Original purpose, original plan
Returning again to the heart of each man
Ruling and reigning again in the Earth
Rejecting the order provided by the curse

My Father, my Purpose, myself as a son
Again all returns to when everything was One
Creation gives creator glory again
So all Yahweh wanted is all that there is.

Maturity

Attaining new thresholds
Arise to new heights
By the glory of Yahweh
We see with new eyes

Growing in judgment
Wisdom and life
We have for the altar
Become qualified

We offer to minister
The fat and the blood
For our Father is worth it
And more than enough

Whatever You ask for
We willingly give
For only by You
Do we have grace to live

But You do not hurt us
For us You equip
All that we need
Now inside of us is

We are empowered
To bring Heaven to Earth
To take back what was stolen
Put an end to the curse

For this we were chosen
For this qualified
For this validated
And thus we're alive

But we now can do this
Only in You
So together we bring back
To creation Your Truth

For we have accepted
Inside of ourselves
Your pure resurrection
And Your place to dwell

We cannot lose it
It's always been ours
For did You not say
We outnumber the stars?

You purposed and planned it
Before You began
So like You we choose
To begin at the End.

The Glory of the Solar System

Like the solar system
Focused on the sun
The light that shines from the center
Draws all things to One

All the planets come to order
In their orbits now arranged
Perfect in alignments
That before time were ordained

And the stars reflect the glory
That is shining in the sun
For of the same substance we are made
And so we're really One

Oh, shining in the darkness
So there's no place without light
Here there is no difference
Between the day and night

The glory of this system
Is the light that always shines
Not because of situations
But because of what's inside

Oh there is a solar system
That is here inside of me
And I will shine within it
So that all the world can see

The glory of the Father
Is the glory of the Son
And the glory that is visible
Is when all becomes One

So we take Heavenly perspective
When looking at the Earth
For from a star's position
There's no longer any curse

For we gaze upon creation
With the light that shines inside
And Reality's the vision
In which we choose to abide

The glory of the system
That is focused on the Son
Knowing His is risen
And that He's already done.

Reigning Truth (Queen's Perspective)

The Kingdom isn't mine
But 'twas given me to reign
But I must see Reality
If I am to ordain

The doubt and the illusions
Have no place inside my mind
So I will choose to cast them out
By the Truth realized

For the Truth did come up to me
And He introduced Himself
And He gave me a choice to be
His reigning Truth myself

When I become His Truth in full
And in His Kingdom take my place
I can bring all things to order
And become the Truth that reigns

All the laws that I tap into
And declare and now decree
All the lines I operate within
From this Truth come to be

But it starts at the Beginning
Oil flows down from the head
If in my metron I want Truth
I must the Truth come to wed

Married to the Truth
With Truth I do unite
Then in all corners of His Kingdom
His Truth will be a light

And become a revelation
Of Truth seeded in creation
Bringing to the surface
His original intention

Back to the Beginning
For the Beginning is the End
In becoming who I really am
Truth's expression I permit

Then the Kingdom comes to order
As the Truth chooses to reign
For when the leader takes his place
That's when the Kingdom's made.

Pitiless

We do not need pity when we have Yahweh's power
We have been called to rule and to reign
We are set in our place and in our hour
We are growing a fruit that remains

There's a clarion call for a people arising
Who take up their scepter in faith
Who more than know the Truth, for the Truth is inside them
Who establish the Truth in its place

We are kings and we're priests of Yahweh Most High
We will choose to be His ecclesia
To stand firm and to reign as the Bride of Christ
It is our time the Truth to reveal

As our feet touch the land to which we were given
Oh, creation on our word awaits!
For if we speak the Truth that's revealed in our vision
The land will reflect what we say

We arise in the force of the Name of Yahweh
For His Word—His Truth—has its own power
It is in His authority and order we reign
As we claim Yahweh's Truth that is ours

With a crown on our head in a place that is royal
It's the day of the Kingdom of Christ
Over each blade of grass and all specks of the soil
We call out the Truth to be recognized!

We establish the Kingdom that Yahweh established
By revealing what's already there
And oh Yahweh's joy at all we accomplish
Nothing else in the world can compare!

Bringing joy to my Father, the joy of my heart
There's no part of our purpose not finished
And oh! The great Kingdom of which I am part
Oh, my Father's great glory and splendor!

Remember
___

Coronation

Stepping up onto the dais
Ready for the crowning
I have received the Word of Christ,
No longer in lies drowning

The crown of the authority
That's coming with my Name
Knowing True Reality
Has allowed me now to reign

The Promise made me before time
Is that I am a king
Reigning over what is Christ's
As I give Him everything

Willingly I take the crown
And lay upon the altar
For the enemy can't cast me down
Or cause me now to falter

I will reign in my Promised Land
In my Eden I will flow
The River of Life is my head
I submit to Him and know

The Truth He called me before time
With Christ I am united
In me, a facet of the divine
Now active and excited

Remembering the Truth of this
That I have authority
To rule out of righteousness
Administering His peace

I take my place in my Promised Land
As priest and as king by faith
I only do what my Father commands
As I receive His grace

And the Father loves the son
And shows to me all things
For only because we are One
Can I even be a king

I take the ring of authority
That's now upon my finger
A signet ring to show all beings
Truth that won't with lies mingle

Knowing the Word of my Father's heart
I can declare and decree
All that He has to impart
So the world becomes Reality

I take the mantle of His Trust
And wear it now with pleasure
For He and I are close enough
That I'm counted a treasure

And I can see more than in part
For He shows me more and more
Of what's inside of His own heart
And what I'm reigning for

Still, humbly I will take my place
Knowing it's only Him
His Word, His Power, His Truth, His Grace
Yahweh is all that is

I take the scepter of finality
And with it I draw the line
For only Yahweh's Reality
Will stand the test of time

I stand firmly with Power's Word
Knowing nothing can me assail
What's spoken in the Beginning is now heard
A Truth that never can fail

My coronation is finished now
Though my regency is not yet done
It is my time to in glory bow
And offer my Father my love

The Kingdom of Yahweh is now at hand
But it has been here all along
Waiting and waiting for a faithful man
Who would be to Yahweh a son.

ABOUT THE AUTHOR

Cassondra Beers is a living representation of Yahweh in the Earth. A wordsmith who is able to see Yahweh in language and has taken her place in her Promised Land, she shares what Yahweh shows her of Him with others. She has had a remarkable journey so far with Yahweh, overcoming depression and anxieties to discover the great joy that Yahweh has for her in her life. One of the ways Yahweh has helped her overcome so much is by speaking to her through writing and poetic expression. The anthologies she writes bring her excitement as she shares this unique facet of Him with you, hoping that you will Remember the special Promise that Yahweh made to Himself through you as each poem is read. Yahweh has always been found to be faithful and she looks forward to where He is taking her next. Cassondra resides in Northwest Arkansas where she spends nine months out of the year teaching and has a spoiled Yorkie named Scrappy. She spends her time connecting with friends and engaging in stories in all forms, including music, movies, and books. Join Cassondra as she shares her poems and revelation on her blogs: *My True Realities* and *Zadokim*.